I KNOW A TRICK WORTH TWO OF THAT

Books by Samuel Holt

ONE OF US IS WRONG
I KNOW A TRICK WORTH TWO OF THAT

SAMUEL HOLT
I KNOW A TRICK
WORTH TWO OF THAT

TOR

A TOM DOHERTY ASSOCIATES BOOK

This two is for Larry and Joe, who know

I KNOW A TRICK WORTH TWO OF THAT

Copyright © 1986 by Samuel Holt

First printing: November 1986

A TOR Book

Published by Tom Doherty Associates, Inc.
49 West 24 Street
New York, N.Y. 10010

ISBN: 0-312-93338-X

Library of Congress Catalog Card Number: 86-50323

Printed in the United States

0 9 8 7 6 5 4 3 2 1

1

Names.

I was thinking about names when it started. I was seated at my double-sided desk, on the side facing the windows—always a bad sign; when I'm serious I face the room—and I was gazing out at West 10th Street in Greenwich Village in New York City, watching the people walk by on the uneven sidewalk across the way. What I was *supposed* to be doing was reading a three-page memo from Zack Novak, my agent, as to whether I (a) should or on the other hand (b) should not appear as a guest celebrity on a new prime-time network quiz show. What it seemed to boil down to was (a) sure, why not, when did exposure hurt an actor? But on the other hand (b) quiz shows haven't succeeded in prime time in years, this one had disaster stink all over it, and they'd already been turned down by a few people at roughly my level of celebrity.

(c) This whole idea was too boring to think about, or read memos about, or make notes about on this yellow legal pad here. Therefore, I was gazing out the window instead, at a sunny spring afternoon in May, daydreaming, watching the people walk back and forth on 10th Street, just below me. I had begun to moon about the differences between Greenwich Village and Bel Air, my other home out in Los Angeles, and it seemed to me the difference was this: In Bel Air everybody is beautiful—with or without the plastic surgeon's help—but it doesn't matter because nobody ever walks anywhere so you never see them, whereas in Greenwich Village there is an incredible range of physical beauty—from a lot to absolutely none—and it does matter, because people walk everywhere and you can hardly keep from looking at them.

This led me to names. Beautiful people have beautiful names—after the plastic surgeon's done, you rechristen yourself—so did that mean plain people had plain names, ugly people had ugly names? That fat man waddling by with his pipe—was his name Gross? The soft-bodied pudgy girl with the bent eyeglasses and straight hair and no makeup— was she Miss Blank? The grim-faced man in the dark three-piece suit and the attaché case and the inexorable stride—Mr. Harsh, I presume.

This led me to think about my own names, the various barks I've answered to one way or another in my life, and into my mind came the line "What's in a name?" Where was that from? Something Shakespeare, I thought; and I call myself an actor.

I was just reaching for Bartlett among the reference works on my desk when the phone rang. Well, Robinson would answer; he was in the kitchen, cleaning up after lunch and just beginning the agonized thought processes that would lead to a decision as to what he'd have for his solitary dinner. He could use the distraction; I went on reaching for Bartlett.

Romeo and Juliet, Act 2, Scene 2, line 43. Juliet says it: "What's in a name? That which we call a rose/By any other name would smell as sweet." You don't have to be an actor—or pretend to be one—to know and recognize that line, of course; all you have to have done is stay awake during high school.

Which I didn't do. I pretty well drifted out of my teens and into my twenties, going to college on a basketball scholarship—I'm six foot six—and dropping out after one year, then being an MP in the Army because that was how they could keep me in Headquarters Group and have me play on the brigade basketball team, then going to work on my hometown police force in Mineola, Long Island, because that's what the Army had prepared me for. What I hadn't been prepared for was that a movie company would shoot some scenes in Mineola, some of us cops would be given small bits to do, and an agent would sign me to an acting contract. Two years and one more agent later, I was hired to play the lead in PACKARD, a kind of private-eye TV series about a famous criminologist, and my life changed forever.

To begin with, PACKARD was a huge success, and only shut down after five years because all of us working on it had grown jaded and tired. (By the fourth year, I was even writing scripts for the show myself, seven of which appeared.) The success of PACKARD made me rich, and the show's reruns will keep me rich for some time to come, maybe forever, but the success also made me essentially unemployable. The public has never seen me in any part other than Jack Packard, friendly criminologist, and producers are afraid nobody will accept me if I pretend to be somebody else. So after five years of intense steady employment, three years ago I became involuntarily retired, at which point I discovered that during the five years of the series I had undergone something of a personality change. I had accumulated good work habits and a strong liking for the job of actor. I had learned from other actors, like my good friend Brett Burgess, and I had come to enjoy stretching myself, solving the problems of my craft. Then, all at once, it was over.

Life can get boring sometimes when you're thirty-four years old, rich, and unemployable.

Zzzz: the intercom. I put down Bartlett and picked up the phone. "Yes?"

Robinson's English-butler imitation spoke in my ear: "A Mr. Hickey wishes to speak with you, sir. He claims to be an old friend of yours—'partner' was the rather Old West way he put it—and says the matter is urgent."

"Hickey? Which Mr. Hickey is that?"

"He says his name is Holton Hickey, sir."

Holton Hickey? I swiveled around in my seat and looked into the surprised eyes of Holton Hickey himself, gazing back at me from the small amber mirror on the side wall. Holton Hickey is *me,* or at least he used to be, back before my first agent changed my name to Sam Holt, as having a more rugged, he-man sort of sound.

As Sam Holt had made his progress through Hollywood and TV land, had Holton Hickey, the cop and basketball player, continued in some other direction, in some alternate universe?

"Hmmm," I said. "All right, Robinson. I'll talk to Holton Hickey."

2

The strange thing is, the voice was immediately familiar. "Hi, partner," he said. "It's been a long time." It was a good strong masculine voice, filled with easy confidence that had maybe been battered recently, causing something tentative to creep in. He sounded to me like someone who wasn't used to rejection, but realized he might be facing it here.

I said, "So you're Holton Hickey, are you?"

"Come on, partner," he said. "*You* know who Holton Hickey is."

"I do, as a matter of fact."

"And if you think about it, partner, you'll understand why I used that name instead of my own."

"Why do you keep calling me partner?" I asked him, getting annoyed.

He sounded pained this time. "I asked you to *think* about it."

So I thought about it. He calls himself Holton Hickey because he doesn't want to use his own name. Because I

wouldn't recognize *his* name? Or because he thinks one of
our phones may be tapped? He calls himself Holton Hickey
because he's trying to tell me we knew each other in the old
days, when that was who I was.

I got that far, but could go no farther, so finally I said,
"Give me a hint."

He chuckled, as though relaxing. "Good," he said. "You
always used to be quick, and I'm glad you still are. We never
could change positions, you and I, because your legs were
too long."

What the hell? There was something vaguely obscene about
that, or overly chummy, suggesting . . . What *was* it
suggesting?

"Come on, *partner,*" he said, leaning on the word, and
then I got it.

Partner. Doug Walford. For almost a year when I was on
the Mineola force we rode a radio car together. And, whereas
most teams alternate between driver and passenger, Doug always did our driving, because my legs were too long and I'd
cramp up in ten minutes behind the wheel.

"Ah," I said.

"Easy," he said, warningly.

Did he think I was about to blurt out his name? If *he* didn't
want to use it, I certainly knew I shouldn't use it. I said,
"Okay, partner, I've got it now. What next?"

"I wouldn't call you at all if I didn't have to," he said.
"And I wouldn't play spy story with you if I didn't have to
do that."

"We know each other," I said. "I remember you weren't
a clown."

"Thanks, Holt," he said, using what is now my last name
but what used to be—pre-PACKARD—my nickname.

"So what do you need?" I asked, wondering if it was
money. I hate to sound cynical, but when you've hit it big

and old friends show up, it usually does have something to do with money.

"A meet," he said. "To describe the problem."

"Where?"

Again he chuckled; I remembered that slightly devilish sense of enjoyment he'd always had. "Do you recall," he said, "where a couple bad boys used to coop sometimes, when life got slow?"

To coop is to take a nap while on duty—a bad and dangerous thing for a cop to do. Nobody does it very often and gets away with it, but we're all human, and there would be days when we both had hangovers or night shifts when we'd both already put in a full day of living, and a thirty-minute nap in the car, parked behind some diner construction site, could make all the difference.

Doug and I hadn't cooped very often, both of us being young and fairly eager and in good physical condition, but for those few occasions we'd found a wonderful hiding place, well within our beat and yet completely out of sight. The Meadowbrook Parkway runs through Mineola and on south to Jones Beach, and at its Mineola exit there's a thick stand of trees inside the off-ramp loop, by the overpass. It was possible to slip a car down in there, between the stone wall of the overpass and the tough springy branches of pine trees, and just disappear from view. Asleep amid the aroma of pine needles, next to the soothing hum of parkway traffic—it just about made me yawn to remember it.

But I stifled the yawn. "I know the place," I said.

"Isn't that nice? You and I know it, and nobody else in the world. And if you go there tonight at two o'clock and nobody follows you, we'll still be the only ones who know it."

Two o'clock? It would take less than an hour to get out there from Manhattan at that time of night. There were things I was supposed to do this evening, but I could definitely get away before one. I said, "And if I were to go there tonight at two o'clock, and nobody had followed me, would I find you there?"

"That's the idea, partner," he said.

3

Out in Los Angeles I have four cars, but in New York, none. For those rare occasions when I need wheels other than a taxi, I have an account with a small limousine and car-rental outfit up on West 56th Street. That night I was having a late dinner at Vitto Impero, the West Village restaurant run by my friend Anita Imperato, and we were having such a good time that when the rental arrived none of us wanted to call it quits.

We were six at table by then, Anita having joined us after her other customers left. The other four were Terry Young, a reporter on the *Daily News,* with his wife, Gretchen, and Bill Ackerson, my East Coast doctor, with a young dancer apparently named Muffin.

Terry Young and I first met eight years ago, when the TV production company sent me east to promote PACKARD, then just starting its run and needing all the help it could get. At first blush, Terry and I didn't take to each other at *all*. I thought he was nothing but a fat slob and a phony, filled with reverse snobbery, and on the other hand he thought I was just another pretty-boy wimp out of Hollywood. Our interview began badly, with both of us tense and hostile and self-protective. I took it for maybe twenty minutes and then I got mad and told him what I thought of him, standing up while I did so for the greater effect my height would have on my words. Instead of crumbling, though, the son of a bitch astounded me by getting mad right back, remaining seated but leaning way back to fire his salvos, letting me know what he thought of effeminate second-raters—I'm paraphrasing, you understand—taking up his time and space in the newspaper for the sole benefit of the meatheads and mouthbreathers—this time I'm not paraphrasing—at the low end of the readership. I replied in kind, we began at that point to reevaluate each other, and we've been good friends ever since.

Terry's not a particularly tall man, but he's big and barrel-bodied. Some of it is fat, but enough is muscle for me once to have seen him knock a man out with one punch. The man had a gun in his hand at the time and had just announced his intention to hold up the bar we happened to be in. Terry decked him, then stood licking his knuckles and shaking his head at his own stupidity. "Now, what did I go and do that for?" he demanded. "As an employee of the *Daily News,* I am not even eligible for its thousand-dollar good citizen award. I have just risked my personal self in public for *free.*"

As for Bill Ackerson, I met him six years ago when I was in New York doing publicity for PACKARD and got food poisoning at a press party. (So did the press; our ink wasn't very good that time.) I only knew two doctors then—the family guy out in Mineola and my Bel Air physician—so Bill Ackerson was recommended to me by an associate producer with PACKARD, and he turned out to be a show-biz groupie in his early thirties, with signed photos of celebrity patients on the waiting-room walls, copies of *Daily Variety* and the *Hollywood Reporter* lying around instead of *Field & Stream* and old *Times,* and a nice line of industry shoptalk.

If he weren't so open and ingenuous about it, Bill could be a little smarmy, but he's cheerful and happy and never does Uriah Heep. Also, through his show-biz clientele, he comes up with an inexhaustible supply of beautiful young dates, such as tonight's Muffin, who turned out to have more of a personality than most, with some very decided views about modern dance: Twyla Tharp, Merce Cunningham, Martha Graham—she'd known or learned from or at least watched them all.

It was a good evening, but then all at once it was one in the morning, the rental car was waiting outside, and my meeting was at two. "Duty calls," I said.

Anita, the owner of the joint, cocked an eyebrow in my direction, saying, "You're sure you aren't three-timing me."

"I wouldn't dare," I told her, which was just about the truth. Anita Imperato and I have had a very low-key on-and-off relationship over the years, never intense enough to ruin the friendship. She knows about Bly Quinn, my steady girl out on the Coast, but that doesn't bother her because, like most New Yorkers, she believes that nothing that happens west of the Hudson matters. A girlfriend within the five boroughs, though, would not be acceptable.

Because of my appointment, I had switched an hour ago to San Pellegrino, a good mineral water Anita had introduced me to, but everybody else was still happily lubricating the conversation with Italian white wine. Still, however reluctant I was, it was time to go. I said so long, and Anita walked with me to unlock the front door. Out on the sidewalk, visible through the glass in the door, the skinny kid from the rental company stood and looked at his watch. Anita and I kissed good-night, briefly, and she said, "Come around when you can stay longer."

"Very soon," I promised, and she unlocked me out and relocked behind me. They would all stay and talk and knock back the Pinot Grigio until morning, and I wished I could stay with them.

The kid gave me the key to tonight's car, a black Mercury Marquis whose front seat would slide back almost far enough for my long legs, and I drove him back up to 56th Street, and kept on across the Queensboro Bridge to connect with the Long Island Expressway.

You will never again know any place in the world the way you know the neighborhood where you grew up. To a nine- or ten-year-old boy, the world consists of driveways, backyards, shortcuts, alleys, routes through fields or apartment-house basements, all the nooks and crannies and corners unnoticed or forgotten by adults. Driving out to Mineola, I was moving into a martial terrain mapped for me by all the adversary games of childhood, in addition to its being the beat where, for a year and a half, I plied the trade of small-town cop.

Doug Walford had seemed to think there was a good likelihood I'd be followed, so I overshot Mineola, leaving the expressway at Jericho and making my way back along quiet deserted suburban streets, surrounded by sleeping commuters. Often I was the only car in sight as I tacked westward by an extremely indirect route.

I parked on a side street, two blocks from our old cooping nest, and walked a block in the wrong direction before making my way to the Meadowbrook Parkway ramp and its comforting cluster of trees.

There was nobody there, and no car. I was two or three minutes early, so I found a dry piece of earth where I could sit with my back against the stone wall of the overpass and wait. Intermittently, cars went by on the parkway; less often, on the town street.

I fell asleep. Well, here were all the old associations—right? Also, I'd done pretty well in the wining and dining department tonight. Also, nothing was happening. I remember my watch telling me it was 2:23, and the next thing I knew a garbage truck went by, changing gears right next to my ear. It snapped me awake, and I took a few seconds to figure out why I was asleep outdoors in the dark with my back against a cold stone wall.

My watch said 2:58. There was nobody there. I stood and stretched, feeling cold and stiff and half asleep and more than a little cranky. What the hell was going on? This couldn't possibly be some stupid joke; it was too elaborate, and there was no reason for Doug to come out of the blue ten years later just to be a wise guy. And it did have to be Doug; in addition to my having recognized his voice, he and I were the only ones who knew about us cooping here.

I walked back and forth, inside the trees, trying to warm up and trying to make some sense of what was going on and thinking about Anita and Terry and Gretchen and Bill and Muffin probably still talking together back at Vitto Impero—probably talking about *me,* in fact—and it seemed to me there were only two explanations: Either this really was some moron's idea of a joke, or whatever Doug had been trying to keep away from had caught up with him. I wasn't sure which explanation I liked worse.

3:07 said my watch. Enough. He isn't coming tonight. Still stiff, increasingly worried, I left the trees and walked directly back to the Mercury. I got behind the wheel, started the engine, pulled away from the curb, and a well-remembered voice from the floor behind me said, "I was wondering when the hell you'd give up. Drive us away from here, will you?"

4

Just south of Long Island, protecting much of its fifty-mile length from the tides and storms of the sea, a series of peninsulas and islands stretches from west to east; Rockaway Beach, Long Beach, Jones Beach, Fire Island, Westhampton Beach, Tiana Beach. At the southern tip of the Meadowbrook Parkway is the bridge over South Oyster Bay to Jones Beach, miles and miles of white sand and whiter parking fields. Late at night the parking fields are almost empty, except for lovers and cops, and on this particular night Doug Walford and me.

We parked the car in a remote dark corner, got out, and walked down onto the beach, where a steady breeze blew in from the ocean. There were stars but no moon, so we could see the beach, but the ocean was formless black. Closing up our jackets, we strolled along the hard sand just above the waves, and Doug told me his story:

"I quit the Mineola force about a year after you did. There was, you know, you remember, a certain amount of chicken-shit, and I just didn't see hacking it that way for the rest of my life. Plus, I grabbed a guy for drunk driving one night, and a week later he came around to my house to say he liked the way I didn't take any shit from him, and he offered me a job.''

"That's a new one."

"Well, he was a big guy. Not as tall as you, but probably fifty pounds heavier, and none of it fat. Harvey Mallon, his name is, and I *didn't* take any shit from him that night. I did a little judo on him, you know, not to hurt, just to control, so that's why he thought he could use me. He has a private-detective agency in New York; he lives up on the North Shore, near Miller Place.''

"You became a private detective?" I thought that was funny, for some reason. Two cops snoozing in a radio car together: one becomes Packard; the other, a private eye.

"That's what I did," he said. "Mostly industrial relations, plant security—"

"Scabs."

"Protecting scabs. There's a difference, but I forget what. Anyway, sometimes Harvey gets embezzling stuff or divorce stuff, and he likes his team well rounded, so we all get assigned whatever jobs come in. I wasn't just Mr. Muscle, in other words.''

I nodded at him. Doug Walford was six two, strongly built, with a wrestler's neck and shoulders, but he also had a brain in his head and decent manners and a pleasing appearance; it would have been silly and boring if he'd settled for being just Mr. Muscle.

He went on: "So it was just the luck of the draw when I got Miriam Althorn, who wanted to divorce Frank Althorn.''

"What were you supposed to do, find girlfriends?"

"No, no, that was all taken care of. The idea was, the divorce is all set, and the agreement is based on a distribution of property, but Mrs. Althorn has the idea Mr. Althorn is fibbing about his assets. If he's hiding cash or jewels or real-estate deeds or bearer bonds or money-market certificates, she wants to know.''

"She wants an accountant for that.''

"She has an accountant, a whole firm of accountants. But when the accountant sees something that confuses him in the paperwork, they need a big fella with presence of mind to go out into the field and see what's there.''

"Okay. What business is Mr. Althorn in?''

"Real estate, it says here. But that's part of my punchline. Althorn is a big builder in the whole New York–New Jersey–Long Island area.''

"Wait a minute,'' I said. "I've heard that name. Althorn Development.''

"That's the guy. Put up a big new building on Madison Avenue a couple years ago, a sports arena out in Suffolk County, hotel construction down in Atlantic City.''

"This guy's property is not going to be easy to keep track of,'' I said. "Not if he wants to hide some of it.''

"That's why the accountants, and that's why me.'' Doug stopped walking, and faced the off-shore wind. "My problem is,'' he said, with heavy irony, "I'm too good at my job. I found out more than I needed to know.''

"Oh, yeah?''

"I found out stuff Mrs. Althorn never knew about and wouldn't want to know about, because if she ever does learn any of that, they'll kill her. They're doing their damnedest to kill *me*.''

"Who is?''

"Some people.''

"Althorn?''

"He'd be one of them.'' He started walking again, and I kept pace with him, our heels sinking into the slightly damp sand. Doug said, "Everybody knows now that Judith Exner was sleeping with a president of the United States and a Mafia chieftain at the same time. Everybody knows now that that president wanted that Mafiosi to kill Fidel Castro. Twenty years after the event, anybody can know anything they want, and who cares. But what I know is what's going down *now*."

"Althorn led you to it?"

"Althorn led me to urban renewal, state government, federal government, everybody cozy in everybody else's pocket. In the other direction, Althorn led me to the guys with the bent noses and the brown tuxedos. And then all of a sudden I turned a page on a document and there I was looking at the third largest pharmaceutical company in the world. And it's at the center of control, it's where all the lines meet."

"Are you talking about dope? Cocaine?"

"No, no, I'm talking about medicine, drugstores, prescriptions, tranquilizers, painkillers, years and years of federal testing and analyzing before you get to put your new wonder chemical on the market. I'm talking about export to the Third World, not import. Clean, clean stuff. Baby formula, plasma, birth-control pills. I'm talking about drugstore chains and the trucking companies that deliver to them and the federal agencies that regulate them and the money moving through the economy and the people who pop the pills into their mouths and knock it back with a little water."

"The pharmaceutical company is mob-controlled, then."

"It's more than that, Holt," he said. A long time had gone by since I'd answered to that name; it gave an additional sense of fractured reality to what he was telling me. He said, "I'm saying that the pharmaceutical company and the mob and the federal government are so linked together they're one outfit. Thousands and thousands of government employees. How many do you think knew Jack Kennedy was sleeping with Sam Giancana's girlfriend?"

"Three," I guessed.

"At most. That's how many government people or pharmaceutical employees or mob soldiers know how deep and beautiful the links are. And that's why, among the very few people who *do* know, there's a decision that the story shouldn't spread. Outsiders who learn too much have to die. Stories about any part of the link have to be sat on until they disappear."

"Listen, Doug," I said, "just tonight I was having dinner with a pal of mine, a reporter on the *News* in New York. He could—"

"Die. Right along with you and me." Doug stopped again, shaking his head, kicking in a frustrated way at the sand. "He'd get all excited about it," he said. "He'd start to do something about it, look for the evidence to back up what I say, and then he'd fall out a window. Or they'd buy him, and get him to arrange a meet with me, and we'd *both* fall out a window. I've had two newspapermen die after they talked to me."

"Doug!"

"Nobody was killed," he said. "Not murdered, not officially. One fatal auto accident, DWI, and one drowning incident in these waters out here. Out by the Hamptons." He shook his head. "Twenty years from now, I could tell my story, get headlines all over the place, maybe even write a book, because then it won't matter anymore. Right now, those people are determined to have me dead, and those people get what they want."

"How long has this been going on?"

"Eight months," he said. "They tried to get me at home to begin with, by means of a hot-water-heater explosion. They got Linda, the lady I was living with, and her daughter, Kerry, but they missed me by about ten minutes, and a friend of mine with the Brentwood Fire Department let me know it was suspicious. Since then, if I go to somebody for help, that person either gets dead or bought. Remember Captain Stasio?"

"Sure."

"They bought him. Or, sometimes people just decide I'm talking like a loony and they back off from me. I *am* talking like a loony, I know it, paranoid delusions, all of that, except it happens to be true."

"So where are you now?"

"Hiding out, but it's no good. See, I know too much but I can't prove enough, so I've got no defense. If they kill me, it's a preemptive strike before I become too dangerous. I had papers in my hand, I saw people together, I had a look at one telephone transcription, but I don't have any of that stuff now, and I can't get back to it. My only hope is to get so much solid evidence that I can go public, and then there's no reason to kill me anymore."

"Revenge," I suggested.

"No," Doug said. "Those guys'll be too busy putting out the fire to think about revenge. Believe me, I've thought this one through."

I personally believed he'd thought it through to a wishful conclusion, but there was no point trying to take away the last hope he felt he had, so I said, "How are you going to get this evidence?"

"I'm not. They've got me so I can't move. But there's a couple fellas I've gotten to know, in other agencies here and there around the country, like Joe Kearny out in San Francisco, and they're doing some work for me. I didn't give any of them the whole story; they only know I want proof about this event or that link. When I get all the answers and put them together, there's the picture."

"And in the meantime."

"It's getting worse, man." We had turned and were walking back toward the car now, Doug's head hunkered down into his shoulders like a turtle, though the wind was neither that strong nor that cold. But maybe it wasn't the wind he was thinking about. He said, "I can't live anywhere very long, I can't talk to anybody very much, I'm going crazy. I *will* be a loony after a while."

"What about money? You aren't working, are you?"

"No, and I was never big on saving for a rainy day either." He stopped and sighed and stared out at the black sea, gearing himself up for something, then turned and looked at me and said, "So far, I've robbed four liquor stores."

"Doug! Jesus!"

"I don't know, I—" He looked confused, addled. "You don't think you'll ever . . . Holt, it was either roll over and die or *do* something. We both know the liquor-store clerk is told by his boss and the insurance company to hand over the cash, don't be a hero, so it was *possible*. Nothing else was possible."

"Doug, this is . . . I don't know what to say."

"Neither do I." We both started walking again, and after a little silence he said, "I'm broke again. But don't reach in your pocket—that's not what I want." With a wry laugh, he said, "It's not as easy as that."

"All right."

"It isn't money anymore. I figure it'll take another six months, maybe even a year, before I get all the little packages of proof brought together in one place so I can go public and get *out* of all this shit. By that time, all right, maybe some liquor-store clerk does want to be a hero and he's got a .32 in the cash drawer, or it's the owner himself, but what's more likely than that is, I'll go round the bend."

"Okay."

"I can't be alone anymore." Once again he stopped and stared at me, daring his own embarrassment and humiliation. "I'm not that tough," he said. "I can't do another year of three motels a week and one armed robbery a month, and never trust a person I see, never sleep without waking up every twenty minutes because it's a strange bed and I just heard a sound. They're succeeding, Holt; they *are* killing me.''

"I can see that," I said.

"I thought about it and thought about it and thought about it. You're the only person I could call, Holt. You're the only person that fills the bill. I can trust you. You can hide me.''

5

"**R**obinson," I said, next morning in the kitchen, "we have a guest."

He looked up from his shopping list. "Miss Anita?" His manner was perfectly neutral, but you didn't need a seismograph to sense the waves of disapproval underneath. His nose, his primary asset during his years as an actor, stood at total supercilious attention, thinner and bonier than ever, simultaneously expressing his loyalty to Bly Quinn, my steady out there in LA, and his utter distaste for the sharp New Yorkese manner of Anita Imperato. On those rare occasions when Anita did stay over, Robinson, who in his seventy-some years of life has graduated from a long career of playing cantankerous butlers and valets to *being* a cantankerous butler and valet, always performed a wonderfully subtle scene of silent disapproval. Fortunately for everybody, subtlety tends to be lost on Anita; if she were ever to discover that William Robinson disliked her, she wouldn't be quiet about it. Robinson, master of drawing-room comedy, would suddenly find himself in a Dead End Kids movie.

However, this time his disapprobation was wasted, as I was happy to inform him: "Not Miss Anita. An old friend from high school." Doug and I had decided on the drive back to the city last night to give him a new identity—scriptwriter Doug Leinster, that being his mother's maiden name and a profession sufficiently arcane and sporadic to explain his having plenty of free time—and a slightly different connection with me: We had known each other in high school, not on the police force. While I drove, Doug had gone through the small vinyl bag he was carrying, holding everything he owned in the world, to make sure it contained nothing to contradict us.

Robinson, downshifting from obloquy, permitted surprise to flit across his semipatrician face before he became again the portrayal of the proper servant. "A school-days chum?"

"He'll be staying awhile. He's had a rough time recently, so take it easy on him."

"In what way would I behave otherwise?"

"That's right," I agreed. "His name's Doug Leinster, and we'll let him sleep as late as he wants this morning."

"Of course," said Robinson, and I left the kitchen to go down to my basement lap pool, the only way I can exercise those particular muscles in New York.

Doing my laps, I found myself going over and over Doug's story. There were specifics he'd just refused to give me, such as the name of the "third largest pharmaceutical company." The life he'd been leading had given him a perfectly justifiable paranoia, so that even I, his only hope, was not to be entirely trusted. Or was he trying to protect me from the wrath of his enemies by keeping me ignorant?

Whatever the case, I'm not completely a stranger to paranoia myself. The Doug Walford I knew was ten years in the

past; it was certainly possible this was a different man now—
less sane, more trouble. On the basis of our past relationship
and the absolute sincerity of the emotions he'd shown during
our talk, I would put him up for a while. However, just to
satisfy my own paranoia, I'd already phoned the *Daily News*
this morning and left a message for Terry Young; let's see
what my demon reporter friend could tell me about Frank
Althorn and mobsters and that anonymous pharmaceutical
company.

"Mr. Leinster is breakfasting," boomed the loudspeaker
in the end wall. My lap pool is the only echo chamber in
Robinson's life these days, and he never misses an opportunity to use it, bouncing his voice back and forth on the pale
green tile walls every chance he gets.

Lifting my head, dog-paddling, I shouted in the direction
of the mike beside that speaker, "I'll be up in a few minutes!" Then I went ahead and finished my laps, thinking this
time once again about names, as when Doug had first called.
"A rose by any other name." I was Holton Hickey and Holt
and Sam Holt and Sam and Packard; Doug Walford had been
very briefly Holton Hickey and was now a variant on himself.

Amateurs change their first names, so they can forget and
not answer when called, and they keep their old initials, for
easier tracing. The sensible thing to do is keep your own first
name—unless it's really unusual—and choose a last name
from your family tree. Playing thus at still being Jack Packard,
I plugged back and forth in the lap pool, the cool water
slopping and splashing beneath the inset ceiling lights, com-
pleting my self-appointed rounds.

Going upstairs in my terry-cloth robe, I heard Robinson's
voice suddenly play squash behind me again, and I grinned at
his coming disappointment when he'd find out I'd been
already out of there and safe from his resonance.

Apparently Robinson had taken seriously my instructions

about going easy on Doug; I found Doug eating a gargantuan breakfast in the smaller dining room, with its view of the back garden and the interesting brick backsides of the houses on the next street. "How are you this morning?" I asked him.

"Almost human," he said, grinning. "Do you really have a swimming pool in the basement?"

"A lap pool. You want to try it?"

"Absolutely. And, Holt—thanks."

"It's just a lap pool," I said. "Feel free."

"You know what I mean." He gestured around at the small room, the view outside, the sounds of Robinson puttering away in the kitchen. "You've got a lot here. You've made it, you're rich, you don't need to take a gigantic risk for some clown you haven't seen in a hundred years."

Yes, I am rich, and yes, I was poor, and there are times when that can make a problem in my dealings with the people who knew me when I had just as little money as they still have. The simplest problem is people who feel envy and just let it show; I simply try, with them, not to look as though I'm gloating over my good luck, and at the same time I try not to apologize for it. The people who feel embarrassed at being envious and then blame me for their embarrassment are harder to deal with; mostly I pretend nothing's going on. As for the people who feel my success means I owe them a debt of some kind, them I simply avoid; there's nothing else to do there.

I'd been wondering what Doug's reaction would be to the contrast between us, and it seemed absolutely free of envy or grudge or possessiveness. It increased his *bona fides* that his only expression was of surprise that, having so much, I'd be willing to risk it. Feeling a bit awkward, I said, "Come on, Doug, there's nothing here I was born with."

"You've got a funny attitude," he said, "but I'm not about to complain. That fellow in the kitchen—why does he look familiar?"

"William Robinson, actor. Used to play snooty English servants."

"Sure. On the Late Show. 'I view the entire proceedings with a sense of deep foreboding.' "

"I think that was another one, but out of the same bin."

"*Does* he view the entire proceedings with a sense of deep foreboding?"

"He would if we gave him the chance. I trust Robinson absolutely, but it was simpler to tell him the high school story."

Doug grinned again. "Total security, eh?"

"Full radio silence."

"Full court press." He abruptly put his fork down and rubbed his face. Looking out at the garden, etched lines prominent beside his mouth, he said, "They're looking for me, Holt."

"They won't find you. And get used to calling me Sam."

He looked at me, considered, nodded. "I see what you mean."

Robinson came in then, to give me a look of disapproval. "*There* you are. Mr. Young telephoned. I attempted to reach you belowstairs."

"I'm sorry I missed it."

"He left his number," Robinson said, handed me a sheet from his memo pad, and turned his most gracious manner on Doug, saying, "Is everything satisfactory, sir?"

"Everything is just great," Doug assured him.

"We have more of everything," the old fraud said, bending slightly from the waist and actually clasping his hands at his waist. "Toast? Eggs? Coffee?"

My God, I thought, he's doing the good witch Glenda from *The Wizard of Oz!* While Doug fended off seconds, I went up to my office, made an appointment to see Terry Young in an hour, and got dressed.

6

Terry Young and I met today in Kenneally's, a reasonable Irish bar and restaurant a few blocks north of the *News* building, where Terry drank beer and ate most of the things listed on the menu while I drank San Pellegrino and picked at a spinach salad and bounced names off him. "Tell me," I began, "about Frank Althorn."

"Don't," he said.

"Don't? Don't what?"

"Whatever it is you're contemplating," he explained. "Don't invest with Frank Althorn, don't rent from Frank Althorn, don't rent *to* him, don't loan him your car, don't invite him to your house. Don't answer his calls."

"You're a real fan," I said.

"When it comes to Frank Althorn," Terry said, "I'll take Genghis Khan. What's your relationship?"

"None."

"Good. Anita was very upset last night."

That troubled me: "Because I had to leave?"

"She *knows* you don't have a girlfriend. On the other hand, she knows you *do* have a girlfriend, out there in Oz, so way down deep in the back of her brain there's a voice that says, 'Maybe.' "

"It really wasn't, Terry."

"Don't convince me, convince Anita."

"Thanks," I said. "I'll do what I can."

"The mystery-man number doesn't play," he said. "You don't have to tell *me* where you were going last night, but I think maybe you better tell her. Did it have anything to do with this sudden interest in Frank Althorn?"

"Yes."

He looked at me, bright-eyed, and waited. I know his reporter's tricks—you let the silence grow long enough, the other guy's going to say something just to hear a sound—so I filled my mouth with spinach and bacon and onion and mushroom, and then chewed, looking right back at him. He drank beer, stuffed a whole lot of food into his face, drank beer, waved the empty bottle at the waitress, swallowed, sighed, and said, "So don't tell me."

"Okay."

"It's *my* brains we're picking today. What do you want to know about Frank Althorn?"

"Is he connected with the mob?"

"Approximately the way Santa Claus is connected with Christmas." Then Terry paused, cocked his head, listened to a replay of that inside his head, and said, "No, strike that. Frank Althorn is not himself actually the member or head of any Mafia family or any other group you could mean when you use the word 'mob.' Do you know what is a *shabbas goy?*"

"Sounds Jewish."

"It is."

"But you're not," I pointed out. If Terry were any more Irish, English troops would occupy him.

"You provincials," he said, shaking his head at me and nodding his thanks to the waitress who brought him his beer. "I was born and raised in Brooklyn, old son," he reminded me, "and even today I could probably do pretty well on the bar mitzvah responses. You know the old saying? If you live in New York, whether you're Jewish or not Jewish, you're Jewish. If you live in Albuquerque, whether you're Jewish or not Jewish, you're *not Jewish.*"

"I guess Mineola must be Albuquerque," I said.

"Very near. Very close by. Orthodox Jews are not permitted to ignite a fire from sundown till sundown on the Sabbath. Turning on an electric light counts as igniting a fire. This causes certain difficulties."

"I can see the possibilities for snags," I agreed.

"So a Gentile—that's you, that's me—a Gentile is hired to do the work in the house that the Orthodox Jew cannot do for himself. That Gentile is called a *shabbas goy.*"

"Why are you telling me all this, Terry?"

"Because it is the only image I can think of that explains Frank Althorn," he said. "Frank Althorn is the mob's *shabbas goy.* He does those things in the legitimate world that they can't do for themselves."

"Ah-hah," I said.

"You may have noticed," Terry told me, "whenever there's a hearing about the ownership of a gambling casino in Nevada or Atlantic City, first there's the hooraw about whether the owners are mobsters. Then there's the hooraw about whether the owners *associate* with mobsters."

"And that's Frank Althorn?"

"It is not. Frank Althorn does not associate with mobsters. He doesn't go to their parties, he doesn't ride in their airplanes or vacation on their islands or attend their funerals.

The FBI does not have one, not even *one,* telephoto picture of Frank Althorn and a known mobster shaking hands on a street corner. That's why I gave you *shabbas goy;* that fellow does not become a Jew, doesn't go to temple, doesn't eat kosher. He remains a Gentile. Frank Althorn remains a clean, solid, upright businessman.''

"Tricky.''

"He seems to find it worth the trouble.''

"He got divorced last year, didn't he?''

"He would have,'' Terry said, looking at me keenly, "but then fortunately his wife had a skiing accident in Lake Tahoe.''

I stared. "She's dead?''

"Six months ago. *Jesus,* Sam, but you've got me curious.''

"Then let's change the subject. What's the world's third largest pharmaceutical company?''

"Judging how?''

"I don't know. Does it make a difference?''

"Sure it does,'' he said. "You could do it by gross sales. You could do it by net worth of assets. You could do it by number of employees. You could even do it by existing patents held. And do you count nondrug subsidiaries?''

"I don't think you can answer my question,'' I said.

"I don't think you can *ask* it.''

"All right. Do you know anything about a man named Harvey Mallon?''

He whooped with laughter, causing heads to turn briefly over at the bar. "By God, Sam,'' he said, "you're all over the lot today!''

"I guess I am.''

"Harvey Mallon has an industrial security company here in town,'' he said. "Goons for your labor troubles. I think he also has a clean side—private investigations, skip tracing, that kind of thing.''

"Excuse me.''

We looked up, and a guy was standing there. About thirty, round eyeglasses, small moustache, suit and tie. He was smiling hesitantly and holding a pen and a memo pad. Knowing what was coming, I said, "Yes?"

"Mr. Holt? My wife watches your show all the time. You know, the reruns."

"Uh-huh."

"Would you mind, uh . . ." He held out the pen and pad.

"Oh, sure," I said. "What's your wife's name?"

"Cindy."

I took the implements and wrote, "Here's to Cindy." Under that I did my two signatures: "Jack Packard," with many flourishes and curlicues, followed by a manly simple "Sam Holt."

"Thanks," the fella said, grinning from ear to ear. "I didn't mean to interrupt—it's just I know she'll get such a kick out of it."

"That's okay," I said. Autograph hunters and starers happen more often away from big cities like New York or Los Angeles, but they're essentially benign people, and what does it cost to give them seven seconds and a signature? Long ago I got over the embarrassment and the sense of being unworthy of all the attention; if *they* think I'm worthy, it doesn't matter what I think.

Cindy's husband left, and I turned back to Terry, saying, "What about Harvey Mallon himself? Apart from his business."

"I don't know a thing," he said. "His company—Harvey Mallon Security Services—shows up in strike stories sometimes; that's the only reason I know him at all. Is it important? I could find out some stuff."

"Not yet. But you don't connect him with the mob, do you?"

"Not before this minute, talking with you. What the *hell* ties all this stuff together, Sam?"

"I'll be delighted when I can tell you," I assured him. "And now there's just one more, a name maybe you could look up in the morgue for me, see if he ever drew any ink."

Terry put down his knife and fork and produced pen and notepad, very like the autograph hunter. "Shoot," he said.

"Douglas Walford. He was on the Mineola police same time I was—ten years ago."

"Is he still there?"

"I don't know. I don't know anything about him since I left Mineola."

He put notepad and pen away, and picked up knife and fork. He frowned at me, then ate awhile, considering me. I also ate, glancing at him, being open and innocent. I am an actor, after all—it says so right here.

Finally Terry sighed and stopped eating. He put down his knife and fork, and said, "I hate it when you lie to me."

"I apologize," I told him. "I hate it, too."

"But you'll stand by the lie."

"For the moment."

"You know nothing about this Walford fella since you left town ten years ago, but you'd rather not call your old buddies on the police department out there and ask *them* whatever happened to good old Douglas."

"That's right."

"Okay." He picked up knife and fork, then paused. "When you do tell me this story," he said, "it's gonna be a lulu."

"I think maybe it will," I agreed.

"And in the meantime"—he pointed his knife at me—"in the meantime, old son, get straight with Anita."

"I will," I promised.

7

Anita was at the cash register, ringing up accumulated lunch receipts. I could see her through the window in the locked front door, it now being almost three-thirty in the afternoon, lunchtime over. Very faintly, I could hear the *ding-ding-ding* of the cash register. She looked absorbed in her work, oblivious of the world around her, and I paused a few seconds before knocking, just to look at her. A good-looking woman. An intelligent, interesting, complex, sometimes irritable woman. Very valuable to me. I knocked on the glass.

I had to do it twice before I managed to recall her from the world of numbers. Then she looked up, frowning, prepared to shake her head violently at some clown wanting lunch at this hour, and when she saw it was me, she looked (a) delighted, (b) guarded, and (c) neutral, all in the space of about a tenth of a second. So Terry had been right; it was time to mend some fences.

She came over, and unlocked and opened the door, saying, "Pick-up or delivery?"

"Delivery," I told her, coming in. "I picked you up a long time ago."

"I picked *you* up, buster," she said, and locked the door. Her eyes kept sliding off me. "I needed one tall enough to put the star on my Christmas tree."

"Don't be mad, Anita."

Her glance ricocheted off my cheekbones. "Who's mad?"

"Okay," I said. "You want to accept delivery?"

"Depends. What is it?"

"The explanation for where I had to go last night. I couldn't tell you in front of everybody, because it's somebody else's secret, but I wanted at least you to know."

Now at last she looked at me directly, without squinting or turning away. "Really? I figured it was like in those sitcoms, where the wifey doesn't know what hubby's up to. I figured you were out buying me a birthday present at two in the morning."

"I was out seeing a friend who's hiding from people who want to kill him."

She gave me a deeply dubious frown. "Run that one again?"

"Let's sit down, and I'll tell you the whole story."

So we did, and I did, and she asked questions and I answered them. I gave her every bit of it, and told her she was the only one who knew: "I had lunch with Terry today, asked him some background stuff on Doug's story, but wouldn't tell him what was going on. And Robinson doesn't know either."

She got up then, probably to give herself time to think. Crossing the room to the service station, she got two glasses and a large bottle of San Pellegrino, brought them back, opened the bottle, poured, sat down, looked at me, and said, "You believe this fellow?"

"So far," I said, and sipped from the glass. "There's still a chance he's gone crazy over the last ten years, or turned into a con man, or who knows what. On the other hand, something apparently Doug doesn't know about: Terry told me Miriam Althorn was murdered six months ago."

"By her husband, you mean."

"By her husband's *shabbas goy.*"

She stared at me. "Good God. Where did a loaf of white bread like you come up with that?"

"From Terry," I said, and then I laughed. "He's Irish and you're Italian and you *both* know the phrase."

"I know what a *gonif* is, too," she said grimly. "What's in it for your pal Doug if he *is* lying?"

"Not much. Room and board for a while. Maybe he could skip out with a couple grand worth of stuff. It's too elaborate, Anita, and there's no real profit in it. Doug could be telling the truth, or he could be crazy, but I have a lot of trouble seeing where he makes anything on it if he's turned into a crook."

"So you'll keep him around awhile."

"That's right. I'll watch over him, and I'll watch him, and I'll see what happens."

"Does he come to the party?"

I was so involved in what was happening right now that at first I didn't get what she was talking about: "Do what?"

"The party. Or are you dropping it? Sam, the *party* I'm catering at your place a week from Monday!"

"Oh, my gosh."

I'd completely forgotten about that. I was throwing a party for maybe thirty people, my semiannual New York bash, the other one being at Christmastime. I was having it on a Monday because Vitto Impero was closed Mondays and Anita

could not only cater but also attend. (It was also on a
Monday because it's easier to make people go home on a
weeknight; on Friday or Saturday, as I know from grim
experience, you're going to have one or two clowns still
hanging around the next day no matter what you do.)

So the party was scheduled for the Monday after next,
eleven days from now. But with Doug in the house, what
should I do? Possible answers crowded into my mind, each
trailing a little cluster of objections:

I could cancel the party; but the invitations had been sent, I
was looking forward to it, and (a touch of Doug's paranoia
reaching me here) such a large and obvious change in my
plans might draw the wrong kind of attention.

So I could have the party as scheduled and simply introduce Doug Leinster, the scriptwriter; but a couple of people
present know scriptwriting and would see through the sham,
and Terry Young would certainly guess who Doug really
was, after our lunch conversation today.

So I could have the party and hide Doug up on the top
floor like the demented cousin in Victorian melodrama; but
someone might stumble on him there, and Doug himself
might not be happy to skulk around like that, and in any case
how would I explain it all to Robinson?

So I could send Doug out to my Bel Air house; but he
didn't know anybody there, it wouldn't be any good without
me to ease him into that world, and a main point was I
wanted to keep an eye on him.

While I was wallowing around in all this confusion, apparently a similar sequence of thoughts had been going through
Anita's head, because abruptly she asked, "Has your pal
shaved yet today?"

"I don't know," I said. "I think so. Why?"

"We'll have to disguise him, so he can be at the party."

"Are you sure that's the way to go? I already thought about it, and—"

"You can't hide him, you can't send him away, and I won't let you call off the party," she said, briskly eliminating all my other possibilities. "You're an actor, aren't you?"

"That's what it says on my passport."

"So you know makeup. Does he have a moustache?"

"No."

"He can have, in eleven days. Maybe a beard too. How about glasses?"

"Doesn't wear them. Okay, I see the point. But Terry's going to tumble."

"Why?"

"All the questions I asked him today."

She shrugged. "We'll tell him, then. Swear him to secrecy, let him know it *isn't* a story whatever his instincts say, and he'll be good. Particularly if we tell him at the last minute, so he doesn't have days and days to brood about it."

"I told Robinson he's a scriptwriter. A couple of people at the party won't believe that, once they talk to him."

She gave me a truly exasperated look. "Come on, Sam, why not? *You're* a scriptwriter."

"Just on PACKARD; that doesn't count."

"It does. And you know scriptwriters. You have a week and a half to give him all the buzzwords and bullshit. By party time, you'll have him sounding like Rod Serling."

I laughed at that, saying, "I'll settle for some anonymous hack, if that's okay with you."

"Sure. So the next question is, when do I meet this joker?"

"You want to meet him ahead of time?"

"Of course. Lay a little woman's intuition on him, see what he looks like, maybe help in the disguise part. What if I made a home delivery tonight, dinner for three, at about ten-thirty?''

"That's good," I said.

"Send a car for me, okay? I'll be carrying a lot of stuff. Dinner for three, and breakfast for two.''

I grinned at her. "You *were* mad, weren't you?"

"I still am, kind of," she said. "But you're gonna be very sweet to me tonight, and after a while I'll forgive you.''

8

Doug didn't like the idea. We talked in the back garden, brick building walls fore and aft, high wooden privacy fences along both sides, and for the first time I had a sense of being hemmed in there. Always before, that garden, with its ivy ground covers and climbing wisteria and meandering slate path and wooden park benches and wrought-iron tables and the impatiens Robinson plants along the path every spring the day we arrive in the city, had seemed to me a comforting oasis in the middle of town, secluded and pleasant. I realized this new feeling of oppression, as though the walls were too close and too high, leaning in on us, was flowing out of Doug in waves of discomfort, affecting me because it was hitting him so strongly. He paced back and forth like something caged in the zoo, shaking his head, staring at the walls and the slate and the vines, all clutching and clinging, green tendrils reaching out as though to choke . . .

"Take it easy, Doug," I said. "You're making *me* crazy."

"Thirty people," he said. "You're talking about thirty people."

"I know them all," I pointed out. "I wouldn't invite them if I didn't like and trust them."

"Thirty people. *One* of them, at least one of them, is gonna have a handle on his back that those guys can reach for."

"If they even know you're here. And there's no reason to think they do."

"Then they will," he said. He still paced, while I sat on a bench, knees crossed, trying to perform comfort and confidence and ease. There's an acting theory, roughly the reverse of the Method, that says if you take the *position* of an emotion, the physical stance that goes with that emotion, pretty soon you'll begin to feel the emotion. From the outside in, in other words, rather than the Method, where you recall an event leading to the emotion you want, and the recollected emotion guides your external posture and appearance. So I sat on the park bench, knees crossed, one arm flung across the back of the bench, portraying a contented householder at ease, enjoying the sunshine on a nice spring afternoon in his own back garden.

It wasn't working very well, not with Doug so efficiently portraying a hunted deer right in front of me. I said, "Doug, we can put this over, believe me. In eleven days, we can change your appearance so you won't be recognized, and give you enough background so you can play a TV scriptwriter in casual party conversation."

"The best thing is," Doug said, "I leave. Maybe just for a couple days."

"No."

"Why not? I'll go stay in a motel for a while."

"In the first place," I told him, "you'll be a lot easier target out there than in here. Besides, where's the security if you keep going out and coming back in? You're in here now, and we can give you a new identity. You'll have to become somebody else sooner or later anyway, Doug; you can't just pull the covers over your head for a whole year.''

He stopped pacing to frown at me. "Is that what I'm doing? Pulling the covers over my head?''

"That's the way it looks to me.''

"Maybe I've been inside this too long," he said, looking away. "Maybe I'm not the best judge anymore.''

"I think that's true.''

He grinned; shaky, but a grin. The leaning walls seemed to recede. "All right, Holt," he said, then stopped himself. "No, wait a minute. All right, Sam. You're in charge.''

"Anita and me," I told him. "She'll be a great help to us.''

That made him shake his head again, looking worried. "First I risk *your* life," he said. "Now, through you, I'm risking somebody I don't even know.''

"Anita is very good at taking care of herself.''

"I think a lot about Linda and Kerry," he said.

I was about to say "Who?" when I remembered from last night. The woman he'd been living with, and her daughter, who had both died in a water-heater explosion. "That won't happen to Anita," I said.

He didn't say anything—just stood looking away, beyond the wooden fence. The walls seemed closer.

9

"Zack," I said into the microphone, "I've thought about this quiz show invitation, and I see the arguments on both sides of it, but I've decided it's not for me. I know you always need reasons, so here they are. In the first place, I don't see myself as a simple display, like the two-headed calf in the jar at the carnival. If I'm going to say yes to anything, it ought to be something to do with my profession. Acting. This isn't—"

A knock on the door. It was a little after ten at night, and I was at last getting around to that prime-time quiz show problem I'd been evading when Doug first phoned. I'd thought there'd be time before Anita showed up to get the damn thing out of the way—producers have taught me over the years that whenever you're stuck on a problem the simplest thing to do is say no and go think about something else—but now here was a knock on the door, just when I was building up to remind my agent that his function was to get me *acting* work, dammit. So I switched off the cassette recorder and said, "Come in," and it was Robinson.

He closed the door behind himself. "Before your friend Miss Anita arrives," he said, carefully avoiding undue emphasis on any particular word, "there are two matters I would like to discuss, if I may."

"Of course. Sit down."

"If you don't mind, sir, I feel more comfortable on my feet."

Recognizing that as a line from one of his movies, I shrugged and said, "Fine with me. You don't mind if *I* stay on my butt, do you?"

"Certainly not." When he chose, Robinson could be absolutely without a sense of humor. He said, "The first subject is Mr. Leinster."

"Yes?"

"Earlier this evening he was wearing eyeglasses."

I had bought clear-glass specs for him this afternoon, on my way back from seeing Anita. "Yes? What about them?"

"He does not normally wear eyeglasses," Robinson said.

"He wasn't wearing them at breakfast, if that's what you mean."

"I *mean*," Robinson said, making it clear he didn't appreciate people who took him for an idiot, "that your friend does not normally wear eyeglasses. He does not have the slightly reddened indentations on the bridge of the nose that so bedevil performers who wear eyeglasses in private life but not when performing in films."

"Ah," I said. "Maybe he usually wears contacts, and lost one."

"Plausible," he said, with a sneer of disbelief. "Earlier this evening, when Mr. Leinster was disporting himself down in the pool, I took the liberty of entering the guest room and looking through his wallet."

"Robinson!" I hoped I looked and sounded as shocked as I really felt.

If I did, Robinson didn't give a damn. "My first observation," he went serenely on, "was that the name on Mr. Leinster's New York State driver's license was Douglas Walford."

"Robinson, you shouldn't have done that."

"I found it striking," this unrepentant reprobate went on, "that this California scriptwriter named Leinster should also be a New York State resident named Walford. However, I found one other aspect of the wallet even more striking."

Oh, well; there was no fighting it. "What was that, Robinson?" I asked.

"The lack of credit cards. The lack of all personal identification other than that driver's license. The lack of business cards. The lack, in point of fact, of virtually all the appurtenances of the gentleman."

"I see," I said.

"You had told me," Robinson said, "that I should, in your phrase, 'take it easy' on Mr. Leinster since he had been going through a difficult period recently. I presume that was the one truthful thing you told me about your friend."

"Oh, Robinson, don't put it exactly like that."

"I know no other way to put it," he said. He was well and truly miffed. "I shan't," he said, "ask for more accurate particulars about your friend. I only point out how difficult it is to keep secrets within a household."

"I see that."

"And I would like to state that I accept Mr. Leinster as Mr. Leinster, and a Californian, and a scriptwriter, and whatever else you wish to make up about him, and I accept him as such because you have vouched for him."

"Thank you, Robinson."

"And now," he said, like someone flipping over a leaf on a clipboard, "about the other matter."

"Robinson, since you already know so much, I'll be happy to—"

"Perhaps, at some later time," Robinson told me, "Mr. Leinster himself will feel it appropriate to confide in me. Until then, don't you think perhaps it's *his* secret to keep or dispense?"

"You're absolutely right," I said. "Punctilious as always."

"Thank you." The old fart actually bowed slightly, before saying, "As to the other matter. Miss Quinn phoned just a few moments ago."

I'd heard the phone, but had let Robinson deal with it. I said, "Why didn't you buzz me?"

"Because I was the one to whom she wished to speak. Are you aware of the pilot script on which she is now engaged?"

"*Helter and Skelter,* isn't it? Something like that."

"That is a close approximation," he said, with a tasting-lemon expression, meaning it wasn't a close approximation at all. "In the story," he said, "there is an old family retainer, who stays on after the new people take over the estate. That is the character about whom Miss Quinn wished to speak to me."

"Oh, very good," I said. "You mean, advice on characterization, the kind of line he might come up with, that sort of thing?"

"Actually, no," he said. Deep down inside that professionally stone-solid face, I thought I detected something very like a smile. "What Miss Quinn wanted to know," he said, "was whether or not I would be willing to come out of retirement to *play* the part."

I stared at him. "To—to what?"

"Perform the role of the retainer Leemy in Miss Quinn's series," he said.

"Well, it's not a series *yet*," I reminded him. "Do they even have a go to shoot the pilot?"

"That is why she telephoned, yes."

"At this hour?"

"Seven in the evening, her time," he pointed out. "She had just returned from her meeting at the network. Casting is about to begin, so she would like my decision at the earliest possible moment."

"Yeah, I'm sure she would." Why did this news irritate me so much? Was it that *Robinson,* even Robinson, could get work, and I couldn't? That it was Bly who'd made him the offer, without even talking it over with me? I said, "Robinson, that would take up an awful lot of your time."

"Yes, of course. But we needn't worry about finding someone to replace me here unless the network—"

"Replace? You wouldn't stay on?"

His thin smile was almost pitying. "That would hardly be practical, would it?" he said. "If the network schedules the program, that is. You yourself have done a weekly series; you know how time-consuming it can be."

"At your age—" I started.

"Precisely what I was thinking myself," he interrupted. "At my age it's too easy to settle into a routine, a life of sameness, devoid of challenge."

"That's not what I—"

"It is by accepting life, in all its diversity," he rolled on, "that we remain vibrant, young at heart. Also, of course, one could expect the recompense to be highly satisfactory."

"But the time, Robinson, the work, you'd be exhausted, you'd—"

"All of these factors must be considered, of course," he said. "And, of course, the change in one's pattern of life. I admit I have grown quite used to our association, and on the whole I am satisfied with it."

"Thank you, Robinson."

"Save the occasional example of a lack of confidence or trust," he went on blandly.

"If you mean Mr. Leinster, Robinson," I said, "you yourself just pointed out it's his secret, not mine."

"That is true. The matter still does, if you'll pardon my saying so, rankle just the slightest bit."

"I'm sorry," I said, but I was filled with too many kinds of gradations of annoyance to make the phrase sound very heartfelt.

"I have promised Miss Quinn an answer by Monday next," he said, ignoring my lackluster apology. "Perhaps at some point on the weekend we could discuss this further, when our thinking has clarified?"

"What a good idea," I said.

"I will ring you when Miss Anita arrives," he said, and bowed himself out.

10

"**W**ell, you don't *look* like a loony," Anita said as she and Doug shook hands.

Doug grinned. The glasses, for some reason, gave him an outdoorsy look, as though he might be something in forestry or the weather service. "I don't know why I don't," he said. "I feel like a loony a lot of times. And you don't look at all like what I'd expected."

"Oh?" They were measuring each other, standing in my living room with me as a fifth wheel and Robinson hovering in the background, waiting to take drink orders. Anita said, "What did you expect me to be?"

"Now that Sam's a big star? Some blond bubbly Hollywood girl. A tennis player."

"Oh, he's got one of those, out West," Anita said easily, and gave me a sharp pointed smile. "Don't you, baby?"

"Robinson," I said, "I'll have Jack Daniel's and soda."

"Certainly, sir." Gliding forward, utterly expressionless, he said, "Miss Anita?"

"Some of the white wine I brought, thanks."

"That sounds good for me, too," Doug said, and gave me a brief apologetic smile. I shrugged; I hadn't told him anything about Bly, so it was hardly his fault.

Robinson went away, and we all sat down, Anita at one end of the sofa, Doug to her right on the dark green morris chair, me a bit farther off in the rocking chair. Anita said, "You know Sam gave me your story, right?"

"Right."

"Tell me," she said, "what did you think of Miriam Althorn?"

I'm sure Doug was as surprised as I was at Anita's chosen entry point, but all he did was grin and say, "I thought she was a greedy bitch. I also felt sorry for her."

"Why?"

"Because she was dumb. She knew what she wanted, but she didn't have the brains to work out how to get it. She used too much makeup, she talked too loud, she pushed too hard, she tried to be tough but she was really very thin-skinned, and all because she was stupid and knew it."

"And Frank Althorn?"

"I never met him."

"All right." Something about those two answers had settled some question about Doug in Anita's mind; she visibly relaxed, sitting back against the sofa cushions and saying, "You know about the party."

"I don't like it," he said, "but I guess I better go along with it." He touched fingertips to his glasses, saying, "But I don't see much use in this disguise thing. I still look like me."

"The glasses are just the start," Anita told him. "You know not to shave?"

"Sure."

"And *I'm* taking over your diet." She grinned at him. "If an Italian restaurant owner can't put fifteen pounds on you by party time, there's something wrong."

Robinson came back with our drinks, and as he distributed them, I said, "Doug, Robinson tells me he searched your wallet while you were swimming."

Robinson gave me a quick betrayed look, but didn't falter in his service. Doug looked at him, and then at me: "That's part of his duties?"

"He was curious, since he noticed you were new to eyeglasses. He tells me he's willing to accept the idea that Douglas Walford of New York is also Douglas Leinster of California, as long as I say it's okay. He didn't ask for explanations."

Robinson, as though our conversation were about the weather or the Broadway season rather than himself, straightened, faced me with his tray at his side, and said, "Will there be anything else, sir?"

"Just wait there a minute, Robinson." To Doug I said, "Robinson knows too little."

"Not too much?"

"Both."

Anita, who had no opinion about Robinson that I'd ever noticed, said, "Actually, he could be a help at the party. Rescue you from uncomfortable conversations, things like that."

Doug looked at Robinson. In a flat voice, he said, "I knew Sam when we were both on the Mineola police. Lately I've been a private detective."

"You were, I take it," Robinson said, "the man who identified himself on the telephone as Holton Hickey."

"That was me," Doug agreed. "Some mob people want

to kill me because of things I know. I need time to get the proof to go public, and Sam's agreed to hide me."

"Mr. Holt is a generous man," Robinson commented, "if sometimes a bit abrupt."

"Leemy is a terrible name," I told him.

"We're considering changing it," he said. "Will there be anything else?"

"Not just now, thank you."

He went away, and Anita got to her feet, saying, "Well, if we're going to fatten you up, Mr. Leinster, we should get started."

11

Later that night Anita did forgive me for having given her several hours of unease, and we spent much of the weekend together, whenever she could get away from the restaurant. Ostensibly she was so frequently at the house because she was bringing so many pastas and pastries to Doug, but while he ate, or read—he was a devourer of newspapers and magazines—she and I had time to ourselves.

On Sunday, Robinson informed me he was going to accept Bly's offer in part. He would play the old family retainer in the pilot, but would not commit himself to the series if the network decided to go ahead. I had decided by then there was no point in envying Robinson his luck, or in selfishly trying to keep him for myself, so I told him I thought that was the smartest thing for him to do: dip his toe in the water, see if he liked it. He agreed, and told me he was now devoting all his time to finding a name to replace 'Leemy.' "It's too bad 'Jeeves' has been used," he commented, and went off muttering names to himself.

Sunday evening Bly phoned, to talk with me directly about Robinson for the first time. "I hope you're not mad," she said.

"Here in the East," I told her, "servant rustling is a hanging offense."

"But what a Ruggles! Imagine Robinson reciting the Declaration of Independence."

"He hardly ever does anything else."

"Don't rain on his parade, Sam."

Several remarks occurred to me. Instead of them all, I suggested "Leemy" be changed to "Meadows," Bly explained why that was a terrible idea, and we both hung up happy. I missed Bly when I was East, her eagerness, her mind full of trivia. On the other hand, I missed Anita when I was on the Coast.

Monday morning Terry Young called. "Doug Walford," he said.

"Yeah?"

"You asked me to check our morgue on him."

"That's right."

"We've got nothing, the *Times* has nothing, but *Newsday* had seven clips."

Newsday, the Long Island newspaper, was the logical place to find references to a Long Island police officer. I said, "Tell me about them."

"The first four are all police stuff—arrests, rescues. Ten, eleven years ago. One heroic rescue of a baby from a burning car, multivehicle collision on the Meadowbrook. Walford was hospitalized for a while with severe burns. The baby lived."

"That's nice."

"Item number five is six years ago, not so nice. Strike at a tool and die plant in Lindenhurst, three private security guards accused of harassing pickets. Your man is one of them, with Harvey Mallon Security Services."

"Okay. That goes with the territory."

"Number six is similar—a trucking company out in Suffolk County that brings produce into the city. Union-organizing efforts. Douglas Walford was riding as a passenger when pro-union people tried to run a company truck off the road. Some shots were fired, by Walford and maybe others. His gun was licensed. He claimed he fired second. Nobody hit, no charges."

"The man knows his job."

"He did, anyway. Number seven is the cutie. Explosion and fire in a house in Brentwood, two dead, mother and daughter. Walford shared the house with them, but wasn't home at the time. A friend of mine on *Newsday* gave me some more. The explosion was suspicious. Neighbors say Walford and the dead woman had been arguing recently, he'd quit his job with Mallon Security not long before the explosion, he was evasive with the Arson Squad, and then he disappeared. There isn't enough for an indictment or a flyer on the guy, but the Suffolk County police would like to chat with him again."

"Hmmm," I said. Doug's story, but with a different spin on the ball.

"Has that helped, Sam?"

"I'm more confused than I was, if that's a help."

"It is," Terry told me. "When you're confused, you haven't made your wrong decision yet. Anything else you want me to do on company time?"

"Not at the moment. Thanks."

"You're welcome. Whenever you want to tell me the whole story, I'll be here. In the meantime, see you next week."

"Next week?" I was thinking about an explosion in Brentwood, mother and daughter dead, and the Suffolk County police interested in talking to a fellow named Doug Walford, who had disappeared.

"You're having a party a week from today, aren't you? Or are you weaseling out?"

"Oh, no," I said. "I'm having the party, don't worry."

"Good. I wouldn't want to miss it."

"You're right," I told him. "This is one party you don't want to miss."

12

At its peak, we afterward figured out, there were thirty-one people in the house, including Doug and Robinson and me, but at its abrupt finale we were down to seventeen. The party started at six, and built up to maximum charge by a little after seven, with people starting to trickle away around eight. During the first hour I kept a mother-hen eye on Doug, but after a while that became impossible, and I just had to leave him to work things out for himself.

Physically, he was fine. Anita's weight-gaining regimen had put fourteen pounds on him, forcing him to go uptown last Thursday and buy new jackets and slacks. The moustache had grown in quickly and well, and so had the beard around his jawline. On the cheeks it was slower and spottier, so on Monday morning he shaved it into a Vandyke, which, in combination with the eyeglasses and the new pudginess, made him look absolutely perfect in the role of Hollywood scriptwriter suffering from writer's block.

Mentally, he was somewhat more worrisome. I had filled

him with TV jargon and lore and shown him some old
PACKARD scripts, and he was a quick study, so that part
was all right, but he was becoming more and more depressed. A couple of his pay-phone long-distance calls had
apparently been very negative, but I think even more than
that was his realization that he hadn't solved anything by
coming to me. I had been his last card, held who knows how
long, and at last he had played it, only to find he was still in
as much trouble as ever, except that the environment of his
prison had improved.

The idea that he was suffering from writer's block came
from Robinson, who'd suggested it to me quietly over the
weekend, saying it would not only explain Doug's very
evident depression but would also justify his not wanting to
talk very much about his work. When I passed the suggestion
on to Doug, I emphasized that second reason, but he smiled
and shook his head and said, "Besides, it's a part I could
play, right? A loser. Somebody who doesn't have it anymore."

"Writer's blocks come to an end," I told him. "So will
this." But I don't think he was convinced.

I'd asked Terry Young to come early, which he did, and I
took him away upstairs to the office, where I gave him a
quick rundown on Doug's story and his disguised presence
here. Terry was dubious about the whole thing. Filling one of
the low-padded swivel chairs at the conversation end of my
office, jacket already rumpled, shirt and trousers already
threatening to part company at his barrel waist, beard bris-
tling with disquiet, he looked like the captain of an equivocal
tramp steamer who's just been informed by the harbor master
that his ship is going to be searched. He said, "You want to
be careful, Sam. My feeling from the *Newsday* guy is, the
cops there think your pal did it."

"They think he might have blown up that house, sure," I
said. "That's what I would have thought, too, when I was on

the Mineola force. I would probably have been willing to bet a couple dollars the autopsies on the victims would show some kind of violence the guy inflicted on them and then blew up the house to cover his crime.''

"Exactly.''

"Terry,'' I said, "if the M.E. had found *one* suspicious element in the autopsies, there'd be a wanted-for-questioning flyer out on Doug Walford right now.''

"Probably so,'' he agreed, with a reluctant nod. "So if he did blow them up, it was for no other reason but just because he'd flipped. Why don't you bring him in here and let us talk awhile?''

"Because he's got a tricky social event in front of him,'' I said. "Three people in the house already know the truth. He's nervous and tense and depressed enough as it is.''

Terry gave me a sly look. "You're worried about his mental state?''

"Not the way you mean. When the party's over, I'll put you together with him, one on one or any way you want it. Fair enough?''

"Fair enough,'' he said, and heaved himself to his feet, no longer worried about his friend but just prepared to enjoy himself. "I saw Anita putting out what looked like ambrosia. Let's get back to it before the proletariat swill it all down.''

Which had not happened. While Terry fell happily on the hors d'oeuvres—Anita was providing only finger food, enough to keep people from feeling their drinks but not enough to make them think they needn't go somewhere else for dinner—I started to circulate, playing host.

Doug was also circulating, though to a far lesser extent. From time to time I caught a glimpse of him, and he was always either by himself in some corner or at the verge of a general conversational group. The only time I saw him talking with just one person it was Terry, which gave me a start for a second, until I saw from their expressions that every-thing was all right. Terry wouldn't go back on our agree-ment, so he was simply scouting the terrain in advance.

By eight-thirty, the host side of me could begin to relax. The party was successful and I'd had at least one conversa-tion with every guest. People had begun to leave, and I could even go over to Doug, standing by himself near the bar, which Robinson manned like a fairly benign Saint Peter at the Pearly Gates. "Doug," I said, "how's it going?"

"Pretty well." He showed a rueful grin, and said, "I could wish I really was that fellow Doug Leinster, writer's block and all."

"That's what makes acting," I assured him. Across the way, an old basketball chum from college days—now a mostly humorless bank executive with a tiny pale wife—was getting ready to go, so I went over to shake his dry hand and kiss her dry cheek.

The people who stayed the longest were, naturally, the ones I nowadays have the most in common with—people in show biz or communications. The food was finished and Anita had become a full-fledged partygoer, and everything was going along fine. I had switched from San Pellegrino to white wine, a sure sign that I felt my responsibility was over for today, and I'd joined an appreciative group around my old pal Brett Burgess, an actor regaling us with stories about his current stint on a New York–based soap opera where he was temporarily employed as a ruthless industrialist with a secret.

Brett Burgess and I started out approximately together, with the same agent and roughly similar appearance, so that we often auditioned for the same part. The difference is that I wandered into acting by mistake, while Brett has always been a serious professional. The other difference is that I lucked into PACKARD and forced retirement at thirty-one, while

Brett has never hit it big and has never stopped working. Neither of us knows which one should envy the other.

"It's ten o'clock. Do you know where your children are?" That's a line on the Metromedia television stations, delivered by a different famous or semifamous face every night, as the lead-in to their ten P.M. news. I'd delivered it myself about three years ago, but tonight it was said, live and at my party—and exactly at ten o'clock, my watch told me—by Bill Ackerson, my show-biz groupie doctor, whom I hadn't seen since I'd left the nice dinner at Vitto Impero to go meet Doug Walford. Bill wasn't here with the opinionated dancer named Muffin tonight, but with a tall svelte striking-looking woman named Vera, introduced as a sportswear designer, who at the moment was off somewhere else. Bill, alone, had come up grinning to the group around Brett, drink in hand, a little shiny around the eyes, to produce the line as though it were the best joke he'd ever heard.

"Hi, Bill," I said. "How you doing?"

"I'm feeling a little squiffed, frankly," he said. "I intend to diagnose overwork in the morning, and prescribe bed rest."

It's ten o'clock. Do I know where Doug is? In the background I could see him, smiling vaguely at a couple of people as he moved toward and then up the stairs. I told Bill, "Join us. Brett's just been giving us soap opera revelations."

"Revelations? I love 'em. What soap?"

So Brett went back to the beginning of his story. While he talked, I kept one eye on the door, remembering my host's duty to say good-bye to anyone leaving, but no one else had left by ten minutes after the hour, when Ann Goodman came worriedly downstairs to say there was someone locked in the second-floor bathroom, who made no response when she knocked on the door.

13

I made two statements for the police. The first included everything I could remember of Doug's story, his reason for needing to be in hiding. The second described the circumstances surrounding my finding of his body, and went like this: "I last saw Doug Walford alive at exactly ten o'clock on Monday evening, May 21. I know the time because someone used the catchphrase, 'It's ten o'clock. Do you know where your children are?' and I looked at my watch. Doug was at that moment moving toward the stairs. I saw him start up, but then I became involved in conversation.

"At ten past ten, Miss Ann Goodman, one of the guests at my party, came downstairs to say someone seemed to be locked in the bathroom, but there was no response when she knocked. I immediately went upstairs with two other guests: Brett Burgess and Dr. William Ackerson. We heard water running in the bathroom, the door was locked, and there was no response when we knocked and called.

"The outer knob of this bathroom door is the sort with a

small hole in its center. An allen wrench inserted into this hole can be used to unlock the door from the outside. I keep such a tool in a desk drawer in my office on the same floor, so I got it, used it, and was the first to enter the bathroom.

"The cold water was running in the sink. The toilet lid was down, and Doug Walford was seated on it, slumped back at an angle against the corner of the room, head hanging forward, hands dangling between his legs, feet stretched out and apart. He was fully dressed. A small black plastic canister with gray plastic lid of the kind used for holding rolls of film was on the floor, along with several amber capsules.

"Dr. Ackerson, who is my personal physician, entered the bathroom after me. I stepped back by the shower and Brett Burgess stood in the doorway, and we both watched Dr. Ackerson examine Doug Walford. 'He's dead,' he said. 'Let me use the phone.' I led him to the phone in my office, where he called the police.

"About the people then in the house. Being the host, I had been keeping an eye on departures, and I can state absolutely that no one left the party between ten o'clock, when I last saw Doug Walford alive, and ten minutes later, when Ann Goodman reported him locked in the bathroom. My valet, William Robinson, who was serving as bartender that night and who remained at the bar with a view of the front door while I was upstairs, and who is making a separate statement, has assured me that no one left the party between Ann Goodman's announcement and the arrival of the police. That means there were seventeen people in the house at the moment of Doug Walford's death. They are as follows:

"Samuel Holt. Myself; host of the party; discoverer of the body.

"William Robinson, my valet, who also lives in the house. Several guests have stated that he did not leave the bar between my going upstairs and the arrival of the police. He had met Doug Walford for the first time approximately two weeks before.

"Brett Burgess, an actor currently working on a New York soap opera; Dr. William Ackerson, my physician; Steve Kramer, a film production manager based in New York; Mavis Fairburn, head of film liaison in the New York City mayor's office; and Agnes Adler, my attorney's wife. These were the people with whom I was in conversation between ten o'clock and ten past ten. None of them left the conversation during that time.

"Anita Imperato. Owner of the restaurant Vitto Impero, caterer of the party, and by ten P.M. a guest at the party. I had introduced her to Doug Walford eleven days before.

"Terry Young, a reporter on the *Daily News,* and his wife, Gretchen.

"Maria Kaiser, a free-lance photographer, who had come to the party with Brett Burgess.

"Vera Slote, a clothing designer, who had come to the party with Dr. Ackerson.

"Morton Adler, my attorney.

"Ann Goodman, a news producer with CBS in New York, who first raised the alarm, and Helen Mayhew, a social worker with the City of New York, working in offices on Court Street in Brooklyn, who came together.

"Jerry Henderson, a director of commercials in New York, and his wife, actress Nora Henderson.

"So far as I know, none of these people, except for William Robinson, Anita Imperato, and myself, had ever met Doug Walford before the party, and they were meeting him then under another identity. Just before the party, I had told Terry Young the truth.

"I never saw the film container or the capsules before finding them with Doug's body. They were not things I had in my house. I understand they contained a lethal poison.

William Robinson, who has been doing some tidying in Doug's bedroom, and at times has laid out Doug's clothes, will say in his statement that he never saw those things among Doug's effects.

"Doug was somewhat morose and gloomy before the party, because the idea of the disguise was unnatural to him. But he handled himself well that evening, and he knew it. I do not believe he was suicidally depressed. I do not believe he committed suicide. I have no suggestion as to how it was done, but I believe the people who have been pursuing Doug Walford learned he was in my house and found a way to murder him.

"I only wish he'd told me more about the secrets he'd uncovered. (See my other statement.)"

On Friday, four days after Doug's death, there was a coroner's hearing. I spoke my piece and so did several other people, including Bill Ackerson, Brett Burgess, Robinson, two police officers, and a city-employed psychiatrist who had never met Doug. The whole thing took less than four hours. The conclusion was that Doug had died by his own hand while suffering depression brought on by delusional paranoia.

Two days later, on Sunday, I flew back to Los Angeles.

14

Once, from Zack Novak's windows, I saw a helicopter go by, among the tall buildings of Century City, built on land that was once the back lot of Twentieth Century-Fox. Being an initial in his firm, Zack rates a corner office, two walls of which are almost completely window, so I got to see the helicopter—white and blue and black, with the word "Police" prominent—make a right turn, fourteen stories above the street, just a few feet beyond the glass. The two uniformed and helmeted and goggled men strapped into its clear plastic bubble looked very intent, staring downward. If they'd glanced my way, I would have waved, just for the sheer unlikeliness of the thing, but I doubt they would have waved back. As it was, the machine slued around the corner of the building, busy and silent, and continued on its mysterious way.

How is it that Zack is an initial in the company? Years ago, when he'd first signed me, Zack was partners in a much smaller agency with a fellow named McCarthy, but shortly

after that, around the time I became Packard, Novak-McCarthy
combined with two other agencies: Career Representatives
Associates (CRA, then, with a home office in London) and
Allied Management. This Frankenstein's monster of agencies
was dubbed Career-Novak-Allied, and all over town people
changed CRA to CNA on their Rolodexes.

In the last few years, McCarthy and a couple of the
original Allied people have splintered off to form their own
management group, CNA bought out its London parent's
interest, and another small agency called Tar-Gray was absorbed, but the essential CNA agency has remained more or
less intact. It represents writers, actors, directors, producers,
and a few composers, and it puts together talent packages for
film and TV programs when possible.

In the meantime, whether or not Zack's trade practices are
fair, they are certainly profitable, and his larger corner office
shows it. There were no helicopters outside the office window
today, my second day back from New York, nothing but the
usual white and silver and black-lined vertical rectangles of
Century City, turning the former Twentieth Century-Fox into
twenty-first-century LEGOs. Inside, Zack's office is domi-
nated by plants, particularly the potted orange tree in the
windowed corner, brushing the ceiling with its glossy dark
leaves and displaying its little hard green fruit. In the corner
farthest from the view was the conversation area, a pair of
low-slung sofas with bulky brown leather cushions and a few
zebra-skin chairs with chrome legs, all grouped around a low
square glass coffee table, on which stood two small pots of
cacti and an African violet.

I was here to talk with Zack about that damn quiz show.
More than ever I didn't want to do it, not after the uninten-
tional and unfunny parody of a quiz show that the inquest had
turned into, but Zack made only halfhearted efforts to argue
with me, so I suppose he too had come around to the idea

there was no way that show could help me. Besides, what he really wanted to talk about was Doug's death, which—because of my connection to it—had generated so much ink that some of it had reached all the way to Los Angeles.

Personally, I didn't feel like talking about Doug's death anymore, not after the inquest and the reporters who'd flocked around for the first few days. In the beginning, I'd refused to talk with them, but then when I saw the police weren't going to treat the death as the murder it was, I briefly considered going public with the help of all those carrion-loving newshounds. Terry Young and my lawyer, Morton Adler, both advised against. They each made the same point—that a TV actor accusing the legal profession of not doing its job would, on the one side, not be taken seriously and, on the other side, merely irritate the people I was trying to goose into action. Of course, they hadn't been goosed into action in any event, so then I regretted not having at least blown off some steam while I'd had the chance. And now it was too late.

Zack said, "I hearken back and hearken back, but I just don't believe you've ever run that Douglas Walford name by me, have you?"

No matter how gloomy I might be, I had to grin at Zack, the only person I can think of who could without strain use "hearken back" and "run by me" in the same sentence. A tall cadaverous man with a gleaming bald head, Zack is always impeccably tailored in dark blue from his London outfitter, and he takes a deep but quiet pleasure in combining a slow and courtly style with the latest business jargon. Now, in response to his "hearken" and his "run," I said, "No, I wouldn't have mentioned Doug. I knew him before I came to California."

"You were in the police together."

"That's right."

I didn't volunteer the story, but I answered all of Zack's
questions, without going into the incontrovertible fact that
Doug had been murdered, in my house, under my protection,
and that nobody was going to do a damn thing about it. The
murderer was home free. Doug had failed, and I had failed. I
didn't go into that because Zack wouldn't have known how
to respond, and it wasn't his problem. He was curious at the
surface level, the way people are, and no more.

Finally we stopped talking about Doug, and chatted about
my alleged career instead. There was a supporting role in a
miniseries that just might be offered, if I was ready to step
down to a supporting role, a thing I'd certainly consider in a
feature film but that might be the kiss of death if I took it in
TV. The offer hadn't been made, so in considering our
response to it we were just blowing smoke together, but at
least it took both of us away from one more rehash of the
death of Doug Walford. It didn't cross my mind, in fact,
until I was driving home to Bel Air, up the long curving
tree-lined restfulness of Beverly Glen Boulevard. And then
what I thought was a kind of silent farewell.

New York was finished, earlier than usual. Robinson and I
were back here, back in the smog and the sun, readapting
ourselves to our California life. (Robinson was working full-
time on the acting job of his life, which is to say the job of
pretending he wasn't excited out of his mind over his potential upcoming role on Bly's pilot.) And here I was, visiting
my agent, dealing with the pool man and the gardener,
making appointments with Karen Platt, my accountant—all
the usual stuff. New York was three thousand miles away,
Doug was rotting in his grave, nobody cared, and that was
the end of it.

Except, of course, it wasn't.

15

"**I**t isn't me, you know," Bly said.

My mind had been off somewhere. I blinked at her, bewildered, and said, "What?"

"Ever since you've been back from New York," she told me, sitting up in bed and half twisting around to get a better look at me, "you've been Achilles in his tent."

"I have?"

"You know you have. And it isn't my fault, or anything I've done. So what gives, Sam? What's the problem?"

Bly Quinn is a fine girl and a good friend and a lovely lover, a beautiful blonde who writes sitcom TV scripts for a living and plays tennis for the sake of her figure and collects stray facts and oddball literary references for fun. I usually love her, in fact I always love her, but it was perfectly true there'd been a bit of coolness between us in the three weeks since I'd been back in California. I'd been aware of it, but I'd just assumed it was because she was stealing Robinson for her pilot. I'd figured that, way down inside, I was

77

probably nursing some dumb grievance, and she was probably feeling a little guilty about it all, and sooner or later it would go away by itself. Did she really want to talk about that? I said, "There's no problem. Everything's fine."

"Come on, my fine Spartan lad. Let's see what's under that tunic."

We were naked, having just had a moderately good mid-afternoon sexual encounter, so this was another of Bly's obscure references. The meaning escaped me, but I doubted it followed from her previous line, so I said, "Achilles wasn't Spartan."

"Give, Sam."

"There's nothing under my tunic but me, lady. Honest."

"*Personne ici* except us chickens, eh?"

"Bly? What the hell is that?"

"Perelman title," she said, dismissing it with a wave of her hand. "Let's talk about why you're in such a rotten mood. And don't claim it's because of Robinson, because we both know that isn't the reason."

"We do? It isn't?" I was genuinely surprised.

"We do and it isn't," she agreed. "It's because your friend was killed, and you didn't do anything about it."

That *did* get my back up. "Do anything about it? Do what about it? I testified at the inquest, I made two statements to the police, I got my lawyer to hassle the DA's office, I made an absolute pest of myself with the cops. What more am I supposed to do?"

"I don't know," she said. "But apparently you think there's something, because this bad mood just won't go away."

I got out of bed, too agitated to stay still. Then, standing there, I didn't know exactly what to do next. Seeing us both naked in the mirror, I said, "You want to go for a swim?"

"I want to talk about Doug Walford's murder," she said. "That was his name, wasn't it?"

I crossed to the dressers, opened a drawer, and took out swimsuits for both of us. Tossing hers to Bly, I said, "It's over. All finished and over."

"If it was over," she told me, "you wouldn't still be mad."

"Goddamn it, Bly, what am I supposed to *do?* The law called it a suicide, the case is closed, there's nothing left."

"Play Packard," she said.

I stared at her, the swimsuit in my hand. "Are you out of your mind?"

"What would Packard do now?"

"Go swimming," I said, and stepped into my suit.

"He would not. He would pick up his buddy's investigation where his buddy left off, because that would be the way to get to the murderer."

"Television scripts," I said. "I'm going swimming, Bly."

"Wait for me," she said, at last getting up and putting on the top of the suit. "I want to come along and nag."

"Won't you let this go?" I asked her. The whole thing was making me nervous and gloomy and angry, and I didn't particularly even want to know why. I didn't want to have to examine my own feelings in this matter, and that's what Bly's prodding would inevitably lead to. I said, "I'm not Packard. I thought you knew that."

"You've been a cop."

"I was never a homicide detective, nor on the organized crime detail. I was a uniform in a prowl car, authority on the street. Drunk drivers and kittens in trees."

"What would Packard do first, in a case like this? And don't say go swimming."

I thought about it. I tried not to, but there it was—I was thinking about it, and Bly could see it in my face. After all, in the last couple of seasons of PACKARD, I knew the character and the form so well I wrote seven of the shows myself.

"Well?" Bly said. She couldn't have found it easy to look stern with her swimsuit trunks in her hand, but she managed.

"There was a name," I said reluctantly.

"What name?"

"He said . . . Christ, Bly, what's the *point* in all this?"

"You won't feel better until you've tried, and I won't feel better until you feel better, so this is selfishness. What name?"

I sighed. "Doug said he had different private-detective friends around the country checking into things for him, each one dealing with a different corner of the story. None of them was going to have enough information to see the whole picture, so what do I gain by chasing them around?"

"Sam? What name?"

Damn, but she was a bulldog once she got going. That was the trouble; she looked like a bit of California fluff, though maybe smarter, but she was really originally Maryland horse country WASP, and those people don't have much experience at not getting their own way. "There's only one I remember," I said. "A guy named Joe Kearny, in San Francisco."

"Oh, good," she said, smiling, stepping into her bikini bottom. "I haven't seen Big Sur in a couple years. We can drive up together."

16

"**R**eady, Robinson?"

"Certainly."

He's not at all a bad actor, I'll give him that. Here he was going off to his first professional acting job in fourteen years, and his usual great-stone-face impersonation had barely a crack in it. A slight sparkle or twinkle in the eye was all that broke through.

We left the house together, me with my overnight bag, him with a garment bag containing suggested costumes from his own wardrobe. Sugar Ray and Max, my two boxers, came loping out of the shrubbery when we emerged. They were happy to see us, delighted when we turned toward the garage; maybe it meant they were going for a ride.

"Sorry, fellas," I said. "Not today." But they came along anyway, just in case I turned out to be wrong.

When I didn't open the garage door in front of the station wagon, the dogs realized they wouldn't be taking a trip after all. They were disappointed, naturally, but they stood around and smiled to let us know we were forgiven. Also, I think they just like to watch motion for its own sake.

Today's choice was the Porsche, a fast little two-seater, which I keep garaged between the Rolls Royce (bought as an investment and almost never driven), and my everyday car, the Volvo. We stowed our luggage in the small space in back, and climbed in.

Robinson in the passenger seat of a sports car looks like the victim in some sort of torture machine in the Tower of London—a tight-lipped torture victim who wouldn't recant or confess even if you strapped him into a Maserati—but today even this physical and cultural indignity troubled him less profoundly. He was damn near smiling as we drove out, honking good-bye to the dogs, who romped down to the gate with us but obediently stayed inside our property as the electric gate opened ahead of us and closed behind us. They continued to stand at alert attention in the rearview mirror as we followed the curve of San Miguel Terrace from its dead end at my property out to Bellagio. Several Bellagios later—Road, Place, Way, etc.—we left Bel Air through the smaller of its two arches (the one Brett Burgess calls the servants' entrance) and headed east on Sunset Boulevard to Beverly Glen Boulevard, and thus through the traffic up and over the hills to the Valley and eventually to Studio City, where I was to switch passengers, winding up with Bly, who had arranged for a company car to take Robinson home when his stint was done.

Through the studio gate I was directed to the visitors' parking lot, where we both climbed out, Robinson now looking solemn, like a child on its way to its first communion. There was something silly and yet dramatic about the moment, and I felt myself impelled to shake his hand. "Knock 'em dead," I told him.

He permitted the thinnest of smiles. "Of course," he said. "I will tell Miss Quinn you are waiting."

"Thank you."

I stood beside the Porsche and watched him walk off toward the low stucco building, the garment bag slung over one shoulder. Would I like a series again, that grind, week after week? God, I'd like *some* work. Something besides PACKARD.

I would miss Robinson if he got the part and if the pilot was picked up for a series and if he decided to go ahead with it. If if if; the Coast is littered with the bones of projects that couldn't fail. In the meantime, at least he was being flattered by this last hurrah, and had something interesting to think about.

He went through the glass door, which semaphored twice, sending no message. I stood in the morning sunlight beside the car. Here in the Valley, it was already hot.

I waited twenty minutes. Partway through, a fellow I'd known on PACKARD, a writer named J.M.J. Harrison, came by on his way to a meeting, and we chatted for five minutes. He told me about all his projects, both actual and hopeful, as people will, and I had nothing to respond. I couldn't tell him about Doug Walford. I did have to tell him about Robinson, to explain my presence there. "Do you ever do guest spots?" he asked me. "Not as Packard, but other stuff."

"I'd be happy to consider it, Jimmy," I told him, poker-faced. "You have anything in mind?"

"Not this second, but lemme think, okay?"

I promised I'd let him think. He looked at his watch and realized he had to go. We told each other it had been too long, and he hurried off to the building, his projects and presentations in the olive-drab ammo case hanging from his shoulder.

Bly finally came out, looking terrific in mostly white and carrying a bright green vinyl bag. We kissed, she apologized for the delay, and at last we got going.

Bly had brought along a small cassette recorder, which she put on the dashboard, saying, "I want you to tell me about Doug Walford again, every detail you can remember. I want it all clear in your mind and solid on this tape."

"Ask questions," I told her.

"All right." She started recording. "Who was Doug Walford? When did you first meet?"

So as we ran out the Ventura Freeway and up through the flat ugliness around Oxnard and the growing prettiness around Santa Barbara and on out onto the Coast Highway above San Luis Obispo, the bright sun picking out every leaf on every tree, the ocean a deep cool blue beneath the warmer lighter blue of the sky, the Porsche frisky and responsive in the beautiful day, I filled two sides of two tapes with the dark details of the life and death of Doug Walford. Somehow, I had become more tightly locked to him now he was dead. He was my Siamese twin, though he'd never been before, and Bly was right: He was the reason for my gloom.

One question Bly didn't ask me, and that I didn't try yet to answer, was this: Why was I going to San Francisco? Was there a hope in hell of solving that murder? Or was Doug merely a grim spirit hooked inside me, giving me no peace, so that I was going to San Francisco only to have him exorcised? And would exorcism be possible? Was Joe Kearny an exorcist?

17

Kearny was a partner in something called Statewide Security & Investigations. He was out when we arrived, but the receptionist recognized me and let us wait in the main office. That's one of the fringe benefits of celebrityhood; when people see you, they think they already know you, they believe they can trust you, and they already have the idea they like you. So this receptionist, who'd been a gimlet-eyed tough broad when we walked in, suddenly thawed into a fan, scrambled around for a clean piece of paper for me to autograph, and told us we could make ourselves comfortable at one of the vacant desks while waiting for Joe Kearny to return. "He won't be long," she promised. "He was just out looking for a couple people."

Looking for a couple people seemed to be the order of the day around here. Although I'd been an actual cop for a year and a half and a security guard on and off and played Jack Packard for so long, I'd never in my life actually been inside a private-detective agency of this kind. We had entered a very large room where a wooden railing separated the visitor from the larger area, where eight or nine desks were scattered around in no particular order. Five of the desks were occupied—by three women and two men, who were steadily, unrelievedly, permanently on the phone, though their conversations couldn't be heard from outside the rail. Inside the rail, I sat at one of the empty desks, Bly took the client's chair next to me, and we eavesdropped blatantly.

The lies those people told! An Oriental woman just behind us made call after call, and she was somebody different every time. She was a hospital, wanting to inform George Hooker that a close relative was seriously ill. She was a lawyer's secretary, wanting to be sure she had the right George Hooker before she sent out the information concerning the inheritance he'd just received. She was from the Board of Education, wanting to know if Amanda Hooker was registered in that school again this year, and if so, what was her current home address? She was from the Unemployment Insurance Bureau, with an additional payment for Clara Hooker, and where should the check be sent? Her manner was brisk but very subtly insinuating, drawing responses out of people like a clever angler drawing trout out of a stream, and once she was sure there was nothing more to be gained from a call, she could cut it off with the precision of a surgeon. I glanced at her from time to time, and though her voice was a wonderful musical instrument, the closed indifferent expression on her face never changed.

Pretty soon, after six or seven calls, the Hooker family was replaced in her efforts by someone named Evangeline Green, but the technique remained the same: Try to find somebody who knows where the subject is now, and give that person a motive for coughing up the address.

This wasn't the sort of private-detective agency in the books and movies. These private detectives weren't looking for murderers; they were looking for deadbeats, and there was no glamour in it. This boiler room was their battlefield, the telephone was their major weapon, and a repossessed car or a payment for two hundred dollars was their victory. Their clients would be banks, furniture stores, landlords. They wouldn't concern themselves with a case, they'd concern themselves with fifty cases and they wouldn't spare a single wasted second or breath on any one of them. And if George Hooker or Evangeline Green were to show up here and start an explanation with this woman, hoping to make human contact, to get some mileage out of the shared frailty of mortals, icicles would form on them within minutes.

It was now about ten in the morning of the day after we'd driven up from LA. We had planned to spend two nights at the Mark Hopkins, so we could give as much of today as necessary to the Doug Walford problem, and not head south again until tomorrow, so we didn't mind the wait, particularly given the quality of the entertainment.

We'd been there about twenty minutes, fascinated—I could see sitcom scripts growing like weeds behind Bly's eyes— when a stocky impatient-looking man of about forty, in a checked sports jacket, with a small bandage on the side of his neck, came in, moving briskly, and said to the receptionist, "Anything?"

"There's—" she started, and gestured toward us.

He saw us, and didn't like it, and interrupted her: "What the hell is *that*?"

"That's Sam Packard, Joe," the receptionist said. "I mean Jack Packard. You know? Sam Holt, he was on TV in that—"

"Yeah, yeah," Kearny said. "You leave them in *there*?" He pushed through the flapping gate in the rail to stomp over to us, glower, and say, "Here for some local color? You will not repeat one word you've heard in this—"

"I'm here to talk about Doug Walford," I said, rising.

He blinked. "Douglas Walford. New York. Harvey Mallon. What about him?"

"He's dead."

"It happens," he said.

"You were doing some work for him."

"I was?"

Celebrityhood didn't cut a lot of ice with this joker. I told myself to take it slow, not to get impatient. It was only natural Kearny would be cautious. I said, "He told me you were one of the people looking into some questions for him."

He squinted at me. "Close buddy of yours, Walford?"

"We were on the force together, years ago, on Long Island."

"Force? What force?"

Enough was enough. "The *police* force, Mr. Kearny," I said. "The regular police force. The fellas who wear the blue suits and tell the truth on the phone."

He grunted. "Come inside," he said, took a step, stopped, looked at Bly, and said, "You an ex-cop, too?"

Surprised, Bly said, "No. No, I'm not."

"Okay," he said. "Come on."

We followed him across the room and through one of the three doorways on the long side wall. He shut the door behind us and said, "Take seats."

It was a small shabby crowded office. Two plain wooden armless chairs faced a small battered desk piled high with documents and forms. A swivel chair behind the desk was also wood and uncomfortable-looking, despite the thin cushion it sported. Before Kearny sat on this cushion, I saw that it had once been pink and had tree-branch lettering that spelled out "I PINE FIR YEW AND BALSAM OAHU HAWAII." Three filing cabinets filled most of the remaining space, crowding over to partially obscure the only window. Outside the window, perhaps eight feet away, was a plain stucco wall the color of Kearny's cushion.

We sat down, Bly blinking steadily like a camera shutter, recording every bit of this scene. I said, "Doug Walford stayed with me the—"

"Hold onto it. Two phone calls first."

As he picked up one of the two phones on his desk, the door opened and the Oriental woman came in. Her arms were lifted as she put on a hat with a feather on it. It did nothing to soften her appearance. "I think I found George Hooker," she said. "Down in Westlake Village."

"Okay," Kearny said. The Oriental woman went out, closing the door, and Kearny made his two phone calls. The first was to an officer of a bank, telling him the car was totaled and burned out and scrap and on a street out in the Avenues. Should he bring it in? Apparently not. The second was to a lawyer, saying that whoever's name might be on the lease, the name on the rent checks was a state senator from up around Santa Rosa. Should he pursue it? That was also apparently not. "My bill will be in the mail," Kearny told him, and hung up, and said to me, "Douglas Walford would not have died in bed."

"No, he didn't. He—"

"My first guess would be suicide." He nodded. "You don't like that, do you?"

"Why would that be your first guess?"

"Because he wasn't getting anywhere," Kearny said, "and he wasn't going to get anywhere, and he didn't know how to stop. He was just flailing away. Things were gonna get worse and never get better."

I could sense Bly's shocked stare on my left cheekbone. I kept looking at Kearny as I said, "Do you mean it's unlikely or impossible that anybody actually was trying to kill him?"

He shrugged. "You go poking around among people who value their privacy," he said, "sooner or later, somebody's gonna decide to try life without you. So my second guess would be murder, and my third guess would be accidental murder."

"The coroner said suicide."

He spread his hands. "So there you are."

"It happened in my house," I said. "Doug was staying with me. Hiding out with me, I guess. He went out a couple times and called you from pay phones."

"Ah hah. You're the safe house. He said he had a safe house, everything was gonna be fine."

"So why would he kill himself?"

"Because everything *wasn't* fine. He was gonna live with you the next forty years?"

"No, of course not, he—"

"Just until he got in shape, right? Six months, a year."

I sighed, and nodded. "All right, Mr. Kearny. After a while, he was going to get depressed, maybe suicidal. He was going to see he'd painted himself into a corner, or whatever you want. After a while. But it hadn't happened yet. Doug did not commit suicide."

He frowned, and looked at the many papers on his desk. There were productive things he could have been doing. He said, "I wasn't as close to Walford as you, all right?"

"Would you tell me what you were doing for him?"

"Not a thing," he said. Then he shrugged and spread his hands, and said, "There was some bank-loan stuff, some port stuff, a Japanese cargo-ship company. He didn't want specifics; he wanted everything. It was a fishing expedition, hoping to come up with something that would connect to something else he knew from somewhere else. Sometimes he'd send me a money order, I'd do a little work on it, send him some photostats to different general deliveries around the

Northeast. I charged him way under the going rate, and then threw in some extra time for the hell of it, but it still wasn't much. I didn't find any wonderful secrets, and I wasn't going to. He never had much money for the job, but even with a blank check it wouldn't have done him any good, and do you know why?"

I shook my head.

"He didn't know what the question was," Kearny said. "The very first thing you have to do in this business is figure out what your question is; then you can go looking for the answer, provided there is an answer, which is frequently not. Walford was floundering around, looking at stray data, hoping he could refine that question down to something useful, and he never made it. How briefly can you tell me the circumstances of his death?"

"Two minutes," I said.

"Go," he said, and looked over my head at the wall behind me.

I didn't waste time looking at the clock with the sweep second hand that had to be there. I just told the story, as briefly as possible, and at the end I said, "How'd I do?"

"Twenty-seven seconds to go. Very good. So now the situation is, Walford was murdered but it was done in a very cute and professional manner, so nobody's investigating. The murderer will not be brought to justice."

"Don't be so cynical," I told him.

He spread his hands again, with something on his face that he probably meant to be an innocent expression. "*I'm* not cynical," he said. "I believe in justice; I hope and pray for it. On the other hand, I don't count on it."

"I don't count on it either," I said. "But if it's important enough, I try to make it happen."

"Well, you're not gonna find Douglas Walford's killer through this office," he said. "He didn't know enough, and I only knew a little tiny bit of it. You could spend the next year going around the country, talking to guys like me, and at the end you'd know maybe half as much as Walford did, and Walford didn't know enough." He nodded at his filing cabinets. "You want his file?"

"You mean to look at?"

"I mean do you want the file. Take it away with you."

I was astonished. "You wouldn't mind?"

"Why should I? Now you tell me he's dead, I'll spend ninety seconds on the phone with a guy on the *Chronicle* to check the *New York Times* obits to verify, and then I'll throw the file away. What do I want with it? I could use the space. You want it?"

"Yes," I said, but I felt foolish as I was saying it. A file of hopelessness, dead ends. Doug hadn't ever found the right question.

When he gave me the file—one manila folder, less than an inch thick, with "WALFORD" hand-lettered in ink on the tab—Kearny gave me some advice as well: "You're not spinning your wheels," he said. "I'd like to think there was somebody who'd hump for me like this. But don't follow Walford all the way down. Do your honorable best, and then quit."

"Don't become obsessive, you mean."

"That's the word." He grinned at Bly. "You're a very pretty girl," he told her. "When you've had enough, distract him."

18

We had lunch in the suite at the Mark Hopkins, partly so we could use the time to look through Kearny's Walford file, and partly because Bly doesn't feel there's enough room service in her life. "You've been spoiled," she informed me. "Do you remember the very first time you ever called room service?"

"Vividly. They were out of the tuna salad platter."

"You don't deserve room service," she decided. "But I do. Gimme that menu."

The view from our high floor atop Nob Hill was north and west, over the Presidio and the Golden Gate Bridge and the bay, away from the showboaty new buildings like the bleached-bone Transamerica tower, all preening themselves downtown like a reunion of school exhibitionists; imagine trying to upstage San Francisco! While waiting for our lunch, we looked out at this view, and considered various ways we might amuse ourselves in town tonight, and tried to remember the last time we'd been up to San Francisco, and wondered idly just what it was exactly that made the locals hate the nickname "Frisco"—anything and everything, in fact, but look at or think about or discuss that folder from Kearny's office.

I think the reason for that, I was just so relieved to be in motion, to be *doing something* about the problem at last, that I was almost giddy with the feeling of a great weight having been lifted from my shoulders. But in the back of my mind, where I couldn't quite bury it, I carried the sneaking suspicion that my *doing something* would turn out to be no more than a furious spinning of the wheels, a false elation on a fool's errand, and I was in no hurry to see that suspicion proved. I was on a high all of a sudden, after a long period of gloom, and I wanted to hold off as long as possible any harsh reality that might bring me down.

As for Bly, she'd been working very hard on *Akers' Acres,* that being the title of her potential series, and if the additional homonym "acher," as in "belly-acher," occurs to you, that's what the creators had in mind. Various elements of *Fawlty Towers* and *Beverly Hillbillies* had been dumped into the sitcom Cuisinart, and it was Bly's task to spread the result on bread.

Well, she'd done it, and now the die was cast. The taping of the pilot was underway, back there in Los Angeles; she'd done all she could for the show and could now dare to turn her back on it just briefly, and she too was feeling that sudden light-headedness that comes with the end of tension. Or, if not the absolute end of tension, at least a temporary time out. If this turned out to be no more than the eye in the middle of the hurricane, with the rest of the storm still on its way, we were still both grateful for the respite.

The waiter had come too recently from the Third World to recognize me—what have I done lately?—so I overtipped him to compensate. He left, and we sat at the white-clothed table he'd set up in the living room of the suite, over by the view. With the endive salad and cold salmon we shared a half bottle of Napa Valley chardonnay, and then at last, over coffee, we spread out the contents of the Kearny folder onto the coffee table.

It wasn't much, by God. Doug's query letters were in there, and I could see what Kearny had meant about his being on fishing expeditions. Doug hadn't asked for specifics, but had just flailed around in the dark, hoping desperately to hit something before something hit him.

Which hadn't worked.

From the look of the file, Kearny had given him an honest return on his dollar, and then some. He'd rooted out bank statements, lists of boards of directors, cosigners of loans, shipping manifests, a whole grab bag of stuff not much more coherent than a clump of papers you might find in a squirrel's nest inside a wall.

The only common thread in all the material was the Japanese shipping company, Okushiri International Forwarding, and one cargo liner of theirs called the *Tsurikake*. And the four cargo manifests from the *Tsurikake* in which Doug had showed the most interest all included shipments of pharmaceuticals or pesticides to Asia, though without the name of their manufacturer.

We finished Kearny's papers and our coffee together. Closing the folder, I said, "Okushiri has offices down on Sixth Street, near China Basin. I guess that's where we go next."

"Mmm," Bly said. She got to her feet, and started unbuttoning her blouse.

I didn't get it. "You don't have to change," I told her. "We should get going."

"Oh, there's time," she said, slipping the blouse off, dropping it negligently onto the closed folder, where it made

a graceful foothill. "It's barely two o'clock," she pointed
out, and reached behind herself to unhook her bra.

"So?"

"So look through that doorway," she suggested, removing
the bra and nodding toward the bedroom. "See how the
afternoon sun is angling in? How it's just starting to?"

"Yes," I said, looking.

"You have a very tense expression around the mouth,"
she told me. "So I'm taking Dr. Kearny's advice."

"Oh, yeah?"

"You see in there?" she asked me, kicking off her shoes.
"Notice how the sun has just started to angle across the
bed?"

"Yes, I do," I said, helping her with her zipper.

"Wouldn't you like to know," she asked me, "how I'd
look, lying in that angle of sun?"

"Yes," I said.

She looked great.

19

"Hi," I said. "I'm Sam Holt."

"Oh, yes," the pretty Japanese receptionist replied, smiling, batting her eyes at me. "I knew you right away." She had a charming accent, a kind of clipped precision in the consonants, each word separated as though by neat and careful mortar.

"And this is Miss Quinn, my research assistant," I added, gesturing at Bly.

The Japanese girl didn't give Bly so much as a glance. Still seated perkily at her desk in the functional outer office of Okushiri International Forwarding, she went on beaming her bright smile up at me, saying, "Pack-odd. I watch you in bed. It is a great pleasure to meet you."

Out of the corner of my eye I could see Bly's amusement. "Thank you," I said, with my own modestly distanced smile and a kind of courtly little head bow. Now *I'm* becoming Japanese, I thought.

The office wasn't particularly Japanese, not the way it

would have been as a PACKARD set. There was nobody kneeling on a mat on the floor, no white porcelain bowls of tea, no delicately painted screens. Instead, here on the third floor of a building filled with maritime-connected businesses, on 6th Street near the docks, there was a standard desk-console for the receptionist with its built-in telephone switchboard, a waiting area off to the right consisting of red corduroy sofas and small square wooden tables, and gray walls mounted with large color photos of cargo ships. And this flirty Japanese girl.

To whom it was time to tell the story, before she went too far—and she would, I knew she would—and before Bly decided to stop being amused. "The reason I'm here," I lied, "is that we're shooting a film in the Bay Area, starting in October."

"Oh, that's exciting!" she said, leaning forward, both elbows on the desk top. She had very black, very bright eyes.

"Two of the scenes," I said, moving right along, "are on a cargo ship. Now, Miss Quinn tells me your company has a . . ." I dipped my head toward Bly, as a pompous ass might dip his head toward his research assistant.

"The *Tsurikake*," Bly said, immediately, deferentially, as a well-trained research assistant might reply to her pompous ass.

"We were wondering," I started, and then stopped, at the sight of the tragic expression that had come to the girl's pretty face. Shaking her head, pursing her lips attractively, she said, "Oh, I am so sorry, but no. It has sunk."

I stared at her. "Sunk? The *Tsurikake*?"

"Yes, *Tsurikake*." The name sounded completely different in her mouth, more like an actual thing. Turning, she pointed toward the waiting area. "That is a photograph of *Tsurikake*."

Bly and I both went over to look at it, a large color picture of the ship seen broadside, with the low hills and jumbled structures of some city on the coastline far in the background; not San Francisco. *Tsurikake* was painted black, with white superstructure and its name in white on the prow. Two flags hung limp at the fantail, neither of them Japanese or American. One would be the company flag, presumably, and the other its nation of registry. Panama? Liberia? Size was hard to guess, but it appeared to be on the small side, a container ship that was kept in good repair without any unbusinesslike frills of color or glamour.

Calling over from her place at the desk, the Japanese girl said, "It was quite a tragedy. It sank with all hands on board."

"Is that so?" While Bly continued to study the photo, I went back toward the desk saying, "How long ago was that?"

"Just last month. I knew the captain. So sad." She looked very pretty when she was sad.

Last month. Around the time Doug was being murdered. I said, "How did it happen?"

"Oh, it sank in a storm," she said. "I believe it was too heavy loaded. Coming this way, you know, our ships carry *so* much weight."

"What's the cargo, usually?"

"Television sets and motorcycles," she said promptly, as though answering that particular question was a normal part of her job.

"And going back?"

"Oh, all different things." She nodded, and patted the desk top. "That is our main purpose here—to arrange for cargo for return. The company would be very distressed if our ships went home empty."

"I can see that," I agreed. "What sort of things do you usually carry?"

"Oh, *any*-thing," she said, and spread her hands in a pretty gesture of helplessness.

"Drugs?"

Her eyes widened. She stared at me in horror. "Oh, *no!*"

"I didn't mean it like that," I assured her. "I meant legal drugs, like penicillin or aspirin. Pharmaceuticals."

"Oh, yes." She nodded her understanding, then shook her head. "I have no idea."

Bly joined us, saying, "Maybe one of your other ships would do. Are any in port right now?"

"Oh, I am sorry," the girl said, looking at Bly for the first time. "The company has a policy that no one is permitted on the ships."

Bly, with an almost imperceptible gesture toward me, said, "But this is a rather special case, isn't it? We're talking about shooting a movie."

"Oh, it would be just impossible," she said to Bly, then turned her sad smile in my direction. "I myself would be thrilled. But the directors of the company . . . You see, they want the ships working all the time, either at sea, or being loaded, or being unloaded, always too busy for visitors. And there is no insurance, either, of the proper kind. We do not carry passengers, you see."

I looked past her at the closed door to the inner office. "Perhaps, if I talked to one of the directors . . ."

"Oh, they are not here. We are only the branch office, you know. Our main office is in Osaka."

"Well, whoever's in charge here, then."

"Mr. Maramuto is *also* in Osaka at the moment," she said. "Conferring with the directors about the loss of *Tsurikake*."

Bly, at last sounding a bit impatient, said, "You mean there's nobody at *all* here with any kind of authority?"

"Oh, no," the girl said, giving Bly a much less personal

smile than the ones she'd been bestowing on me. "No one who could go against the orders of the directors."

I said, "When will Mr. Maramuto be back?"

"Perhaps next week," she said, but with doubtful frown lines creasing her smooth-skinned brow. "Or perhaps the week after."

She was good, all right. I glanced over at that inner door again, knowing there was no way short of pulling a gun that would get me through that ordinary gray metal flush door and face to face with whoever might be inside. This smiling flirtatious girl, with her easy sadness and gossipy casualness, knew her job well and did it superbly. She was there to keep nonessential visitors away from the bosses, and that's just what she did. "I'll probably phone," I said, though I knew I wouldn't.

So did she. Smiling, she said, "I will recognize your voice." She made that an invitation.

"I'm flattered," I told her.

We all said our good-byes, Bly the only one of us showing any overt irony, and outside, as we went down the metal-railed stone staircase, she gave me an arch look and said, "Well, there's your chance to change your luck."

"Oh, shut up," I said.

She laughed and laughed and laughed.

20

According to the original plan, we'd head back for Los
Angeles tomorrow unless something really compelling came
along to keep us in San Francisco, so after striking out at
Okushiri International Forwarding, Bly and I split up—she to
go to the main library on McAllister in the Civic Center, I to
spook around Okushiri's warehouse down by China Basin—
and then we'd meet back at the suite to compare notes. I
stayed with her until we found a cab, then kissed her, put her
in the cab like a present I was sending somebody, and stood
watching until it turned the corner a block away. Then I
turned and headed for the waterfront.

Everything in San Francisco is clean, washed by the damp
ocean breezes and the frequent fogs. Even the waterfront, in
the cool spring sunlight, had a fresh-paint look to it, though
at least the workmen I saw still had the traditional layer of
grime that comes from working with goods in transit. I went
to the address for the warehouse I'd found in Kearny's
folder, and found a completely unidentified cinder-block build-

ing painted gray, set back from the street, and with a tall chain link fence around it, topped by razor wire. No name on the building, not even a house number, though from the numbers on the nearby buildings this had to be the address.

Railroad tracks were off to the right. Standing on the gravel between the fence and the building were four parked cars with California plates and one large rusty green LTC container, the kind of thing that would be filled with sixty television sets and stowed as a unit into a ship's hold, or put on wheels to become the rear part of a tractor-trailer rig.

At one corner of the fence was an electrically operated gate, but no bell or other way to signal the people inside. This was the receptionist's stonewalling without the smile; go away, was the message, we don't need to meet anybody new.

This area, south of Market Street, is well off the normal tourist trails, so I had the streets pretty much to myself as I wasted ten minutes walking around Okushiri's warehouse trying to find a way in. Then, as I was about to give up, and was pondering whether or not to wait for the owner of one of those cars parked in there to come out, a pair of guys came ambling around the corner ahead of me and swaggered my way, both carrying beer cans in small brown paper bags, but not drinking from them. They were laughing and joking together in a very swashbuckling way, like extras in a pirate movie. They weren't as tall as I am—very few people are—but they weighed more, and it wasn't all beer belly. They were both in scuffed steel-toe workboots, faded jeans, and T-shirts. One T-shirt was green, and it read, in black, "Death From Above," while the other was red, with a cartoon of a bearded biker driving his motorcycle over naked women. They were clean-shaven, with thick dark unwashed hair. One of them wore a gold button earring.

And they were goddamn sure of themselves. I wasn't on guard, saw no reason to be on guard, and if they'd just abruptly turned on me, they might have done some real damage right away. As it was, though, they wanted to play games, so they stopped in front of me, blocking the sidewalk, talking kiddingly to each other:

"Here's a great big mother-fucker, isn't it?"

"Great big pansy, *I* think."

"You think so? You mean we shouldn't oughta be afraid of him?"

"I tell you what *I* think. *I* think we oughta just tromp the mother-fucker for being so ugly."

"He is ugly, he is that."

Meanwhile, I had noticed that the beer cans in the brown paper bags weren't beer cans. They were short lengths of heavy iron pipe about the size of beer cans, which would be just small enough for those guys to make a fist around. Anybody they then hit with that fist would know it. And it looked as though I was the person they intended to hit.

Was this a message from Okushiri? "I was just leaving, fellas," I said, in case it was.

"He even *sounds* like a pansy."

"An ugly pansy."

"I just can't stand him anymore."

"Neither can I. I say stomp the shit out of him before he revolts anybody else."

Their grinning mouths and red-rimmed beady eyes turned toward me, they stepped forward with those iron-holding fists cocked, and a police patrol car pulled gently to the curb beside us.

This was so unexpected that for three or four seconds we all just went on doing what we'd been doing: them advancing and me bracing myself, trying to decide whether to lunge at them both or try to grab just one and use him as a battering ram against the other. Or maybe the thing to do was turn around and see if it was possible to outrun them. The result was, we didn't so much stop as merely run down, like a film projector when the cord has been pulled from the outlet, and at the end of it we were all three in somewhat odd positions: them holding alleged beer cans up next to their right ears, apparently listening to the foam dissipate, and me leaning forward in a crouch, knees and waist and elbows all flexed, hands out as though playing an invisible piano. In those positions, we all turned to look at the police car.

The driver was male; the rider, female. It was the female who was on our side, with a pretty but blunt-featured no-nonsense face under her police cap as she lowered her side window and said, "Any trouble, guys?"

We all shifted into more amiable and normal positions. "No, *ma'am!*" said one of my friends. He smiled, the way he would have smiled at teacher twenty years ago, and folded his arms over his chest, obscuring both the non-beer can and "Death From Above."

"I was just asking . . ." I said, and stepped closer to the police car, and bent down to talk to my fair rescuer, resting my hand on top of her chariot, "just asking these fellas, the way to Market Street. I think I must be lost."

She gave me a flat look. "I think you must be," she said. It was one of those rare times when I had no idea whether I'd been recognized or not. She pointed through the windshield. "You go that way. Just go straight ahead, you can't miss it."

"Thanks a lot," I said, and tapped the patrol-car roof, and straightened. "Thanks, guys," I told my swashbuckling friends, with a big grin. "I appreciate the help."

"Any time, pal," said one of them, with a glint in his eye and a glint in his teeth when he smiled.

I walked around them and headed at a moderate pace toward Market Street. When I looked back, as though casually, a block and a half later, my two friends were gone but the patrol car was still there. They'd be able to see me all the way to Market Street, where I'd have no trouble getting a cab.

Lucky they'd come along when they had.

It *had* been luck, hadn't it?

21

The Japanese girl had lied.

That was the sum and substance of Bly's story, once we got together again back at the hotel. The details of the lie were like this:

First. She'd said the *Tsurikake* had been coming from Japan when it had sunk, and therefore had probably been overloaded with television sets and motorcycles. But the truth was that the ship had been four days out from San Francisco, in open water, on its way to Bangkok, and not heavily loaded at all.

Second. She'd said the ship had gone down in a storm. But there had been no storm. The newspaper reports Bly had found at the library said the weather had been good, there had been no word of trouble from the *Tsurikake*'s radio prior to the end, and from the few bits and pieces of wreckage found afterward—coupled with the abruptness of the ship's end—the theory was that an explosion had taken place on board. Since there was no reason to suspect sabotage, the further theory was that something had gone wrong with the engines or some other machinery aboard.

"So now what?" Bly asked me.

"That's the question, all right." In late afternoon, the sun made the suite too hot, so we'd closed the lace curtains and moved around now in a faint glow of amber air, like a scene in a musical. But nobody was singing.

"There's *something* going on," Bly said. "That's a definite trout in the milk."

"There's a whole lot going on," I agreed, ignoring whatever that reference had been. "But what is it, and what does it have to do with us? There's nothing in all this to connect with what Doug talked to me about that night on Jones Beach. Nothing about pharmaceutical companies, nothing about Frank Althorn, nothing to link up with any of the people who were at that goddamn party."

"That's what it comes back to," she said. "That goddamn party."

"Yes."

"In a way, I wish I'd been there. But there has to be *some* kind of link, Sam."

"Why does there?" I asked. "We don't even know what we're looking for. Doug knew and couldn't find it, so what chance do we have?"

"There's something with that shipping company," she insisted.

"Maybe," I said. "Maybe they sank the ship themselves, to get rid of evidence or somebody who knew too much or for the insurance or for who knows what reason. Or maybe it was an accident, and it doesn't connect to anything. Those two jokers who offered to hand me my head could just have been a couple of waterfront tough guys, out for a good time."

"Too many coincidences," Bly pointed out, "and too

many things that don't fit right. Like those police just happening to show up at the right second.''

"Sure. Does that mean *they're* in on it? And if so, what is it they're in on?''

"Maybe they were part of a stakeout.''

"On what? Me? The tough guys? Okushiri? Or some completely unrelated cocaine deal going on down the street?''

"I just have the feeling . . .'' she said, pacing the living-room floor while the amber shadows grew warmer and darker with the end of afternoon, "I just have the feeling we're at the edge of something.''

"Bly,'' I said, "if you look into *anything* deeply enough, you'll find anomalies, you'll begin to think there's something going on, there's too many coincidences. We don't even know what Doug *wanted* with Okushiri. Maybe they're innocent bystanders, and he wanted information because of somebody else. A brother of one of the board of directors, something like that. We don't *know*.''

She sighed, frowning at the curtains, biting her lip. Her own golden coloring was enhanced in this amber light, making her look beautiful and powerful, like something in Wagner, but her expression was of helpless frustration. "We can't just stop,'' she said. "By golly, Watson, the game's afoot!''

"Yeah? What do we do next?''

"Couldn't we . . . I don't know, couldn't we break into that warehouse tonight, late at night?''

"If we want a head full of shotgun pellets,'' I said. "And if we want to commit several felonies for no better reason than that a murdered man once asked some questions about a legitimate company.''

She paced and paced, shaking her head. "In a script . . .'' she said, and her voice trailed off.

"I know, I know. In a script, someone would knock on the door there and say, 'You want to know about Okushiri?' and tell us the whole story. I think I wrote that scene once myself.''

"Or we *would* find a way to break into the warehouse at midnight,'' she said, "and there wouldn't be any guards around, and in no time at all we'd stumble right across the evidence.''

"Evidence of what? The link between Frank Althorn and the third largest pharmaceutical company? The ties between the mob and Washington? *That's* the story Doug was working on, and we're way the hell and gone out on some tiny remote corner of it that doesn't make any sense at all.''

"Something,'' she said, and sat down on the sofa, and opened yet again that folder from Kearny's office.

There was nothing in there, and we both knew it. I turned away and went over to the phone and called l'Orangerie and made dinner reservations for tonight, and when I looked back at Bly, she was shaking her head at the papers in the file. "Well?'' I said.

"There's nowhere to go,'' she said. "There's nothing concrete, there's nothing *real*.''

"That's right.''

"Joseph K did not know the charges against him.''

"No, he didn't.''

"There's no *suspects*.''

"And nothing to suspect them of.''

She looked up at me, torn and reluctant. "It's over?''

"It's over,'' I said.

22

Down through Big Sur. Beautiful weather, not much traffic. The Porsche twisted and turned along the cliff road; down below, the ocean shattered itself over and over against the rocks; and the Walford folder was stowed in my overnight bag in the back.

But that isn't what we talked about. Mostly, we talked about *Akers' Acres,* about Bly's love of the craft involved in writing for television sitcoms, and her amused and sheepish attitude toward the finished product, and the drive was mostly very pleasant.

We stopped for lunch at Ventana, eating at an outdoor table, high over the sea. I was suggesting alternate names for Robinson's character—Lancaster, Cruikshank—when Bly said, "But it isn't over, Sam."

I looked at her, feeling betrayed. "Come on, Bly," I said. "Lay off."

The fact was, if it weren't for the manner of Doug's death, I would now have said he *was* delusional, as he'd suggested

113

about himself that first time we'd talked. Conspiracies and cover-ups at every turn, with nothing linked to anything else, no comprehensive overview, nothing to get one's hands on. But in being murdered, Doug had established his *bona fides* against all the evidence. Somebody had hired or arranged or ordered that he be put out of the way, which meant there had to be fire somewhere behind all this smoke. But I knew now there wasn't the slightest chance I would ever find out who that somebody was or what was being hidden. So what was there to do? Nothing.

Bly shook her head. "You can't leave it alone, you know," she said. "I'm sorry to come fling these naked pigeons in your face, but there it is."

"Naked what?"

"Pigeons. The Doug Walford—"

"Now, wait a minute." Usually I let Bly's references just roll on by, but not this time. "*What* naked pigeons?"

"*The Big Knife,* Jack Palance to Ida Lupino: 'Why do you come fling these naked pigeons in my face?' Meaning she was telling him an unpleasant truth, and he didn't want to hear about it."

"So what unpleasant truth don't *I* want to hear?"

"That you aren't finished with the Doug Walford murder. It still bothers you."

"Well, of course it still bothers me, but there's nothing to *do* anymore. We proved that yesterday."

"I was thinking," she said, ignoring her lunch and looking out over the ocean far below. "I was thinking about what that man said. Kearny. He said Doug Walford had never figured out the right question. Maybe that's what's happening to you, too, and why we spent so much of yesterday wasting our time with that shipping company."

"I don't see it," I said. "I have a very simple question: Who killed Doug Walford?"

"But what does that question *mean?* Do you want to know who paid for it?"

"Who caused it, who killed him—that's right. I don't see your problem."

"I think," she said, "you're doing a Scarlett O'Hara, except tomorrow never comes."

"Say it out, Bly. What are you talking about?"

"Here's the question, phrased the right way," she told me, and sat up straighter to deliver it, looking me in the eye. "Who violated my hospitality and betrayed my friendship and brought evil into my house?"

"Shit," I said.

"That's right. Sam, I was thinking about it last night, and I just kept remembering that man Kearny saying how important it was to get the question right, and I knew *you* were doing the question wrong, and now we both know why. It was a houseful of friends, and—"

"I know," I said. "All right. That's what I've been trying not to look at, you're absolutely right. People I know, I like, one of them—"

"That's why you came back here," she said, "months ahead of schedule. *One* person betrayed you, but you don't know which one, so they all look a little bad and sinister right now, and it was too uncomfortable to be around them. Too depressing. Who's a human being, and who's a pod?"

"Invasion of the Body Snatchers."

"So now you know what you're going to do next," she said.

"Maybe the trouble with the right question is," I said, "that that's the question I don't want the answer to."

"So we'll rephrase it just once more. Who are the ten or fifteen people who *didn't* play you false? Wouldn't you like to know the answer to that?"

"Yes," I said.

23

It was strange being in New York without Robinson. *Akers' Acres* had kept him out on the Coast, and a house has a different feel to it when there's no one else there, when that other person is *not* two rooms away or up one flight. First I called the answering service to say I was back and they shouldn't refer callers to the Los Angeles number anymore. Then, after unpacking, I went down to the lap pool to work out my travel stiffness, and for the first time it felt creepy and eerie to be down there, in an enclosed green tile box underground, down underneath an entire tall and heavy and empty house. I did half the laps I'd intended, put on my terrycloth robe, and went upstairs to phone Brett Burgess, who was still performing the mad industrialist in that soap opera. But it was just after eight in the evening, he was already out, and I got his machine. "It's Sam," I told it, "back in town. Give me a call when you can."

What now? My stomach was still on California time, three hours earlier, but sooner or later it would be dinnertime even in California, and I didn't want to go to Vitto Impero and sit around with Anita. Not tonight.

I'd worked it out on the plane. There had been seventeen of us in the house when Doug had been killed. I'd been talking with five people during the time when the murder had to have taken place, so they were all out of it. Robinson had not left his post as bartender during that time—several people had sworn to that—so he was also out. That left ten people, at this point, who had the opportunity. And Anita's name was on that list.

Well, who was I going to cross off? Terry Young, my reporter friend? Maria Kaiser, Brett's photographer girlfriend? If I started saying, "Oh, no, it couldn't be her, it couldn't be him," I'd have to cross off every name and forget about it. The whole point was that the killing had to have been done by someone I wouldn't believe possible.

A couple of the people on the list I didn't know particularly well, but they'd been brought by people I did. Helen Mayhew, for instance, the social worker out of Brooklyn, had been brought by Ann Goodman, the TV producer I've known and liked for almost ten years. The fashion designer Vera Slote had been brought by my show-biz groupie doctor, Bill Ackerson. And just thinking about these people's occupations made the whole idea of them as professional killers absurd: fashion designer, social worker, doctor.

Anita, owning an Italian restaurant in Greenwich Village, and Terry Young, a reporter with the *News,* were in fact the likeliest of them all to know or have some link with people in organized crime.

I didn't want to see Anita just yet or any of the other people on that list. But just as strongly, I didn't want to be around people who hadn't been at that party, who had no connection with what went on there. What it came down to, I wanted to spend the evening with one or more of the five people I'd been in conversation with at the time of Doug's death. So when Brett was unavailable, I called Bill Ackerson, and happily he was home.

"Sam! You're back in town? Terrific. For how long?"

"A few weeks anyway," I told him. "It was kind of a last-minute idea, so I'm sort of at loose ends."

"Have you had dinner?"

"I ate some things on the plane."

"Then you'll want some actual food. Shall we break bread together? I bet you have tons of fresh West Coast gossip."

"Not really," I said. Bill Ackerson loves show-biz gossip, the raunchier the better. "Well, just one thing," I went on, remembering a tidbit I knew he'd like. There was a well-known male star who was a deep-closet homosexual, a fact I'd told Bill a couple of years ago. More recently, as I'd also told Bill, this man had decided he wanted to come out of the closet, strike a blow—if you'll pardon the phrase—for gay rights, and time his announcement to the release of his next movie. All of his friends and advisors and agents had been arguing against the idea, but he was adamant. He felt it was something he could do for the cause, a statement he could make, and that he was a big enough star so the public would go on accepting him in romantic hero roles afterward. The new news I had for Bill was that he'd finally been talked out of the idea, by one line from his attorney, which had cut through all the theory and all the sentimentality and all the politics to the bare-bone truth: "Wait another ten million dollars, John."

"*Love* it!" Bill said. "My God, that's where it is, isn't it?"

"That's where it is," I agreed. "Where do you want to eat?"

"What's wrong with Vitto Impero? I haven't seen Anita since that night."

I'd been prepared for that: "I want to get out of the Village, Bill, I'm too much in the same old rut all the time. What's good up in your neighborhood?"

He pondered. "Steak, French, Chinese, or Italian?"

"How French?"

"*Nouvelle* but nice."

"I'll take it."

24

They served me San Pellegrino, but reluctantly, and I had to remove the circle of lime from the glass. All around on the other tables, Perrier with lime stood at place after place, like awards.

The food was good, the wine excellent, the linen snowy, the ambience quiet, the service correct, and Bill in fine form. He had more show-biz gossip than I did, being more interested in the subject, and kept me laughing through much of the meal.

Eventually, however, as was inevitable, the conversation turned to Doug Walford's death. "That hit you pretty hard," Bill said.

"He was in my house. He'd asked for my protection."

"On the phone this evening, you sounded a little depressed. Is it still bugging you?"

"I suppose so. The thing is, Bill, it had to be one of the guests."

He nodded. "I was thinking the same thing myself."

I shrugged, and sipped San Pellegrino. "So it's bound to be depressing, isn't it?"

"If it's true."

I frowned at him. "If what's true?"

"I'll tell you where my own thinking went on this," he said. "Who among the people in that house that night is a killer? None of them."

"One of them."

"Which one? It's not possible, Sam."

"What's the alternative?"

"The coroner's verdict was right."

I stared, not believing he could say such a thing. "Suicide? Do you really believe that?"

"I don't believe either choice," he said, looking at me very intently. "I don't *believe* it one way or the other. Whether he was murdered or he killed himself both seem impossible to me. But it's got to be one or the other, so there we are."

"It wasn't suicide."

"Can you be absolutely positively sure of that?" Bill leaned forward over the remains of his dinner, very earnest. "This thing is bugging you too much, Sam, I can see it is, so think about it. Think about the possibility that *nobody* is a murderer, that Doug Walford is a suicide."

"No," I said, shaking my head. "I'd like to believe that, Bill, I really would. You don't know how much easier that would be, but I can't."

"He wouldn't do it, you mean? You knew his moods, all that?"

"No, leave that to one side. Where did those pills come from?"

"The capsules? He had them hidden somewhere."

"Not in my house, he didn't. Robinson was very interested in that mystery man. He went poking through all of

Doug's very few belongings. The film tube full of capsules was not there.''

"Then he got them that day. He kept them in his pocket. Besides, Sam, how do you kill somebody with capsules? If I was up there holding a gun on him, saying, 'Take these capsules,' he'd know he had nothing to lose if he hollered instead. Or was he supposed to think they were something else?''

"As a matter of fact," I said, "we had that situation on PACKARD one time, so I can tell you exactly how it was done.''

He looked startled. "Remind me.''

"He never took any pills or capsules at all. Somebody came up behind him and injected the poison into him, then arranged the scene so it would look as though the capsules were the method. I asked the medical examiner, after the inquest, if there'd been any capsule casings in Doug's stomach and he said there weren't, but there wouldn't be, because they have to dissolve first. One needle mark in the back of an arm or somewhere could look like a mosquito bite or like nothing at all.''

"Jesus," he said, nodding, looking at me with wonder. "You're right, Sam, it could have been exactly that way.''

"So it could be either a man or a woman, because Doug didn't have to be overpowered.''

"I'm sorry you told me that," he said, reaching for his wine. "I was very happy thinking it had to be suicide.''

"It was murder.''

He drained his glass. "I was just remembering that famous old Sherlock Holmes dictum about eliminating whatever's impossible. What you're left with, however improbable, is the truth. But what if nothing's left? What if all you have is two impossibles? Murder or suicide.''

"Then," I said, "you have to eliminate whichever one is

impossible in the greatest number of ways. Doug wouldn't, couldn't, and didn't commit suicide."

"I believe you," he said. "So that's why you're back, is it?"

"I feel foolish about it," I admitted, "but yes."

"Packard's on the case."

"That's why I feel foolish. What I need is one of our writers to give me the rest of the script."

"*You* were one of the writers," he pointed out.

"I gave Packard easy cases."

He sat back, looking off, touching his lips with his napkin. Then, as though working it out for the first time, he said, "I'm not a suspect."

"That's right."

"Brett was talking about the soap opera. You, me, who else was there?"

"Six of us."

He nodded slowly, thinking it over. "By God, maybe you could narrow it down. Maybe you could."

"I'll try, anyway."

"Let me volunteer myself," he said. "For anything needed. Medical particulars or anything else. Bounce theories off me. Put me to trailing people. Anything."

"Thanks, Bill. I appreciate that."

"I'm not just being polite," he said. "I mean it. You don't want to be alone with this thing, Sam. It'll drive you crazy."

"Welcome aboard," I said.

25

It wasn't a late night; Bill had office hours in the morning. I got home a little after eleven, checked with my answering service, and there had been two calls. The first was from Brett Burgess, giving me a number I didn't know to call tomorrow afternoon, and the other was from Anita. The operator quoted her message: "Your place or mine?"

Of course Anita would have to find out, one way or another, that I was in town. Probably Brett had called the restaurant when he hadn't found me at home.

Anita just cannot be the killer, I told myself. Never mind how it can't be anybody else, it can't be *Anita*. I phoned her second number, the one that rings both in the restaurant and in her apartment upstairs, and when she answered, I said, "How about your place?"

"It must be just about dinnertime for you, isn't it?"

"I ate with Bill Ackerson."

"Oh." I could guess her thought sequence: He comes to

town unexpectedly, he doesn't tell me about it, he has dinner with his doctor. "Everything all right?"

"Everything's fine," I said. "The way you mean it, everything's fine."

"How do I mean it?"

"Do I have any dread diseases. I do not."

"So the way I don't mean it, everything isn't fine. Come over here, clown, and let's sort this out."

"Yes, ma'am."

"If you make it forty-five minutes from now, come upstairs."

"I will," I said, and I did. Only the night lights were visible through the windows of Vitto Impero as I walked across Abingdon Square. I unlocked the door beside the restaurant, and went up one flight to Anita's apartment, in the rear half of the second floor. Her tenants—she owns the building—occupied the other five apartments in the four-story building.

Anita's place has one anomaly: It contains no kitchen. An interior flight of circular stairs leads down to the restaurant's kitchen, if the need should ever arise—and it's also her route to and from work—but with her general disdain for food, no kitchen of hers would get much workout anyway. The question of ice and mixers is resolved by a small refrigerator in the outer part of the bathroom.

The large square onetime kitchen at the rear is now Anita's bedroom. She excavated down to the old fireplace and got it working again, and instead of the rear windows, she'd put in two sets of French doors leading to the tarred roof back there. That roof, created by the fact that the first floor extended twelve feet farther back than the rest of the building, she duckboarded and leveled and turned into a terrace alive with greenery. Wisteria and Virginia creeper now fringed it all, converting the nonview of other building backs into a city approximation of a forest glade. The shrubs and flowers out there blended with the houseplants filling the bedroom itself, linking indoors and out. The terrace and the bedroom and the rest of the apartment show a delicacy of touch in the decoration that always surprises me, "delicacy" not being the first word that comes to mind when I think of Anita.

For instance. I walked in, and there she was in the small vestibule between living room and bedroom, hands on hips, saying, "Okay, pal. You want to tell me right away and get it over with, or do I have to pull teeth?"

"Anita," I said, "let me come in and close the door, all right?"

She shook her head and went away to the living room, and I shut the door and followed.

The living room is done in pale greens, with light but comfortable furniture and plenty of places to put your feet up or a glass down; a room for talk, for easy conviviality. And apparently also for the third degree. "Sit," Anita said, pointing at a chair, "and explain yourself."

"In a minute," I said, and kissed her. I put my arm around her and picked her up off the floor while we kissed, because I knew it would irritate her. Then I put her down, grinned, and said, "First the warm welcome, *then* the bamboo shoots under the nails."

"All right, all right," she said, disengaging, trying to hide the fact she was flustered. "Do your aw-shucks number and grin at me and all the rest of it, and when you're finished, I'm still waiting for my explanation."

"It was a last-minute idea to come to town. Spur of the moment."

"Sam, sit *down*," she said. "I hate to crane my neck back like this."

So we sat. I refused the chair she'd pointed to, and took the love seat, and after a brief hesitation she joined me.

Looking me in the eye without having to crane her neck, she said, "Is this because of Doug Walford?"

"Yes."

"He's why you left all of a sudden, and now he's why you're back all of a sudden."

"That's right."

"You still think he was murdered, is that it?"

"What do you think, Anita?"

She shook her head, frowning, looking away from me across the room. "I've been going over it and over it, and I just don't know. It didn't *seem* as though he was in that kind of mood, and I agree with you about the problem of where did the pills come from, but if it was murder, Sam"—she turned her troubled frown toward me—"if it was murder, have you thought about what that means?"

"Yes."

"It had to be a guest of yours, somebody at the—" Then she stopped, her eyes widened, and she reared back a little, saying, "Is *that* why you didn't call?"

I sighed, knowing this was going to be a rough passage. "I don't believe you had anything at all to do with Doug's death," I said. "But your name is on the list, yes."

"It's on the list." There was no expression at all now in her eyes or in her voice.

I took the quarter-folded piece of paper from my pocket and handed it to her. "The people at the party."

She unfolded and studied it awhile. Then, without looking up, she said, "Why are these names crossed out?"

"That's the group I was talking with at the time. Plus Robinson, who didn't leave the bar. What other names would *you* cross off?"

"Mine."

I nodded, though she wasn't looking at me. "I want to," I

said, "but then where do I stop? Do I not cross off Brett? Terry Young? *Gretchen* Young?"

She tapped the list. "Who's this Vera Slote?"

"Fashion designer. Bill Ackerson brought her."

"You don't know her, in other words."

"No, but I know Bill, and I understand she's pretty famous in her field. But if she's the mob's professional killer, and they got her into my house with Bill's help, then Bill had to know what he was doing. That much couldn't be coincidence."

"Jerry Henderson—who's he?"

"He directed a couple of PACKARDs, the last year. He moved back to New York recently; he makes more money directing commercials here than episodes there."

"So how well do you know him?"

"Fairly well. Not as well as some of the other people."

"Nora Henderson. His wife?"

"Yes. And an actress, called Nora Battle. Does dizzy blonde character bits."

Anita studied the list some more, then finally sighed and shook her head and looked at me. "You didn't want to think about it, that's why you left."

"But it stuck in my craw."

Carefully folding the paper, she handed it back to me and said, "Let me offer you a drink now, okay? If I'm the one who poisoned Doug Walford, and if I know Packard is on the case, which means sooner or later I'm bound to be found out, then I'll poison you, too, right now, and your worries will be over. If you survive the drink, you can run a faint pencil line through my name. Is it a deal?"

I had to laugh. "It's a deal."

"Hemlock and soda?" she asked, getting to her feet.

26

I had already been poisoned, though. Suspicion is almost the worst of poisons, isn't it, staining and altering everything you see or do or think. Your beliefs become riddled with it, like a progressive disease. And the most corrosive part is, it's yourself you can no longer trust, your judgments, your convictions, your emotions.

I believed in Anita, I was not a big enough fool to doubt her, and yet suspicion kept me awake most of the night, playing out scenarios in which her ex-husband applied pressure, or in turn had pressure applied to him, or she was threatened with the loss of the restaurant, or a thousand other ifs. Wherever Anita might be vulnerable—and everybody is vulnerable somewhere—the suspicion fed, growing and moving in my mind.

Beyond the French doors, above the lacy vines, it was a clear beautiful mid-June night in New York, and I saw most of it. On the bed, Anita asleep beside me, I lay awake, forced to think about my suspicions, but at the same time finally made fully aware of my anger. Whoever had done this, whoever had murdered a man in my house, had also dirtied his friendship—or her friendship—with me, and had soured my own friendship—or love, sometimes—with everyone else on that list.

I'd been angry about that from the beginning, refusing to think about it. I'd been enraged, but I hadn't had anything to do with all that anger so I'd simply gone away, pretending it didn't exist. Then, when Bly had pushed me, I'd tried at first to pretend the anger could be resolved by solving Doug's case, either learning what he had learned or discovering his murderer's employers. It was only now, when I'd been half-driven back to New York, when I'd been unwillingly brought to see what had been done to my relationship with *Anita*, that I was becoming aware just how angry I'd been all along.

I'll find you, I thought, as I lay there unable to sleep. I'll find you, and you won't be Anita, and I'll make you sorry you ever claimed to be my friend.

One thing the insomniac knows: First light will bring sleep. It did again this time, and I was very groggy when Anita finally roused me, poking my ribs with her sharp knuckles and saying, "Are you going to lie there all day?"

Sunshine never reached her terrace till midafternoon, so looking out the French doors wouldn't help. Thrashing around on the bed, squinting at the light, unwilling to be awake and to have to face all this again, I managed to ask what time it was, and when Anita said, "Ten o'clock," I groaned and sat up and said, "Let's just skip today."

"Nine-fifty-four, to be exact," she said, looking past me at the digital clock. Fully dressed in blue jeans and wordless T-shirt, she was seated on the foot of the bed.

I reached for her, saying, "Anita, what I need is tender loving care," but she shook her head and got to her feet and retreated toward the doorway, telling me, "Oh, no, you

don't. Get dressed and come downstairs. I'll give you coffee,
and we'll have a nice talk."

"I don't want a nice talk."

But she was gone. So I got up and dressed myself and
went out onto the terrace for a minute to feel the soft air and
try to get some oxygen into my clogged and achy head. Still
not fully awake, I went back inside, sat on the bed, phoned
my answering service, and was told that at nine-forty-seven
this morning I'd received a call from Harvey Mallon.

Harvey Mallon. He had been Doug's employer, at the time
when Doug had learned the too much that had eventually
killed him. Harvey Mallon Security Services. I phoned the
number Mallon had left, and a receptionist led to a secretary,
who, after a pause, turned me over to Mallon himself. So this
was no small operation; I gave up the mental image I'd had
of an outfit similar to Joe Kearny's out in San Francisco.

Nor did Mallon sound anything like the gruff-spoken Kearny.
A buttery syrupy voice on the phone said, "Mr. Holt, I know
you're a busy man."

Then you know something that isn't true, I thought, but
what I said was, "I admit I was surprised to get your
message."

"A friend of ours in San Francisco told me you were still
troubled about what happened to Doug. So am I, you know."

"Are you?"

"Oh, yes," he said. It was an evangelist preacher's voice,
radio-rich, full of sincerity and reassurance; I automatically
distrust such voices. He said, "I was hoping we might be
able to get together, talk it over. At your convenience, of
course."

"Today would be very convenient," I told him.

"Well, that would be just fine. I'll be in the office all day,
so you pick the hour."

I was supposed to call Brett this afternoon, and it was now

10:17 according to this red-numbered clock-radio in front of me. Also, I should spend some time with Anita. "How about noon?"

"Perfect," he said, and we told each other we were looking forward to the meeting, and we both hung up.

So Joe Kearny had called Harvey Mallon, had he? So maybe I was stirring something up after all.

27

Anita and I had coffee and juice and a lot of vitamin pills washed down with San Pellegrino at the front-window table of the closed restaurant, Vitto Impero not opening for lunch until eleven-forty-five. I told her about the unexpected Mallon call and we speculated as to what it might mean, and then she asked me what I was going to do next about that list in my pocket. I said, "After I see Mallon, I'll call that number Brett left."

"Brett? I thought his name was crossed off."

I looked at her. "His girlfriend," I said. "Maria."

She nodded, slowly, then gave me a sympathetic look. "Poor baby, what a job."

"Yes, I know."

"Do you? You have to go to people you like and people you love and throw mud on every one of them, just to see if it sticks."

I paused, my coffee cup in my hand, but when I studied

her face, there was nothing in it but sympathy. I said, "Is that what I did to you?"

Instead of answering that question, she asked one of her own: "Is that the only way to handle it? Go from one old friend to another, treating everybody like suspects?"

"I guess so. Just like good old Packard."

"Never mind Packard." She shook her head at me. "He wouldn't be involved with all the people in a personal way like this. He wouldn't see them as friends. The question is, what would Sam Holt do?"

"Hide his head in the sand as long as possible," I told her. "After that, I'm not sure. Ask dumb questions, maybe."

"Like what? You didn't ask *me* any questions."

"Well, it felt too awkward," I told her. "That's another way I'm not like Packard."

"Ask me now."

"All right. Where were you between ten P.M. and ten-ten the night of the party, and who were you with?"

She shook her head at me, saying, "That's what you're going to go around and ask everybody?"

"Why not?"

"Because people don't remember where they were at a party," she explained. "You were the host, you were watching the door and the clock. Also, you were nervous about your friend, so you were watching him. But most people don't go to a party to remember it."

I said, "Anita, who were you talking to when the word came downstairs that something was wrong?"

"Robinson," she said promptly. "I was getting a drink."

"How long had you been there?"

"A minute or two, waiting. Terry was in front of me."

"Did you go over to the bar together?"

"No. I was talking with Nora Henderson and then Jerry Henderson came over and Nora told him it was time to leave, so I finished my drink and went to the bar. I hate that conversation, you know, where the wife tells the husband it's time to leave. I know it's necessary, but I hate it. I used to have to *do* it all the time.''

"How long were you talking to Nora?"

"Just a few minutes, maybe five."

"And before that?"

"I have no idea," she said, and shook her head again. "Most people are going to have no idea, Sam."

"One will know," I told her. "So I'll just have to keep asking."

28

The easiest way for me to get around Manhattan, unfortunately, is with a limo and chauffeur. There's no place to park in midtown, for one thing, and a famous face like mine attracts the wrong kind of attention if I try to hail a cab, so whenever I have an appointment beyond walking distance of home I call the car service on 56th Street—the same place I got the black rental Mercury the night I met Doug.

But this car was a dove-gray Cadillac, with four gold plush seats in the rear, two facing forward and two back. The chauffeur was my usual driver, a heavyset white-haired Irishman named Ralph with a cheerful competent manner and a serene disregard for celebrityhood. He'd driven me in from Kennedy Airport last night, and now he grinned and said, "No rest for the wicked, eh?"

"That must be it."

A TV set, telephone, and tiny bar were between the rear-facing seats, but I had no use for them. I spent the time between Anita's place and West 51st Street going over what little I knew about Harvey Mallon.

An unusual man, apparently. Nine or ten years ago, he'd been driving home across Long Island while under the influence, had been stopped by a cop (Doug), had put up an argument and been subdued, and a week later had shown up at the cop's house, not to continue the argument or get even but to offer the cop a job. A strange combination of realist and romantic, judging from that.

The offices of Harvey Mallon Security Services, on the fifteenth floor of a building at 6th Avenue and 51st Street, emphasized the realist side, reminding me that both Doug and Terry Young had suggested that most of Mallon's clients were the kind of people who need armed guards to deal with their labor troubles. The outer office was expensively anonymous in neutral shades of gray, and the receptionist—young, but not particularly good-looking—made a flashy show of her efficiency, as though it were some tricky sport like basketball. She recognized me, but made a point of not making a point of it.

I waited no more than three minutes before a very short girl appeared, this one better looking, who smiled and asked if I were Mr. Holt. When I agreed I was, she asked me to follow her, and led the way into a short corridor with abstract paintings on the left wall and doors to small offices on the right. This was a far cry from Joe Kearny's operation out in San Francisco.

The girl opened a broad dark-wood door at the end of the corridor and ushered me into an office that might have belonged to a prosperous attorney or advertising executive. But the man crossing the carpet to greet me, smiling, hand outstretched, had the plump sleekness of a successful celebrity surgeon.

No, he didn't. As we shook hands, as his radio announcer's voice said, "Happy you could spare the time," as his confident guileless eyes met mine, I realized he wasn't soft at all. He played at being soft, as some men play at being ignorant and some women play at being physically inept. Harvey Mallon's softness was a filmy padding over steel.

"Where Doug Walford is concerned," I answered, "I can spare all the time you need."

"Yes, that's what I'm afraid of." His smile turned rueful, and he gestured to an L-shaped arrangement of brown leather sofas to one side, saying, "Have a seat. Coffee? Diet soda?"

The girl who'd led me here stood waiting in the open doorway, smiling. Half to her and half to Mallon, I said, "Do you have any mineral water?"

"Perrier?" he asked.

"If that's what you have."

The girl said, "We have Poland Spring, San Pellegrino—"

"That's what I'll take."

"Fine," Mallon said. "And I'd like a Tab, Laurie."

Laurie went away, closing the door. The social niceties dealt with, we each took a sofa, and I noted the magazines on the glass coffee table: *Business Week, Barron's, Soldier of Fortune.* That last was meant to be comic, of course, a joke waiting like a land mine for the rich soft client to stumble over. A subtler version of the same joke was in the antique chess sets displayed on the étagère nearby.

Mallon said, "I know you're busy, Mr. Holt, and I know damn well *I'm* busy, so let me get to the point."

"Fine." That he didn't start right off calling me "Sam" was a mark in his favor.

"Douglas Walford was murdered."

"That's right," I said, a bit surprised that I hadn't had to argue the case.

"In your house."

"Right again."

"Pissed you off."

"More like a slow burn, actually."

He grinned and leaned back on his sofa. "David Susskind once told me," he said, "never to expect brains from an actor, but you're no dummy."

I answered his grin. "Maybe that's why I'm not working." I knew the name-dropping was a business habit and had nothing to do with me. Probably Mallon had been one of a group of private detectives or security people or suchlike on the Susskind interview show one time, and ever since then he'd find some way to work the connection into opening conversations with potential clients and other people he wanted to impress. It probably worked with clients, but I was the wrong fella to drop names on, which Mallon would have realized if he'd thought the situation through.

Laurie came back, then, with a round silver tray containing two highball glasses, a small silver ice bucket with tongs, and a can of Tab and a bottle of San Pellegrino. She put the tray on the coffee table, smiled at us, and left. Mallon and I busied ourselves with ice tongs and so on, while I reflected that even the executives I'd known in the television business wouldn't have been able to bring off this pretentious a treatment of a can of Tab with such self-assurance.

After one sip of his soda, Mallon leaned back again, smiling, pleased with himself or me or the situation. "I used to watch your show, you know," he said.

"Oh?"

"It wasn't very realistic." Then he shook his head, still grinning, to take the bite out of the remark. "A lot of fun, of course. I enjoyed it a lot. But I'm in the business, you see."

I said, "Mr. Mallon, are you going to tell me not to poke my nose into Doug's murder?"

He sat up, smile disappearing. "Certainly not. How would I presume to tell you what to do or not to do?"

"I just thought that was where we were heading," I said, because I still thought that was where we were heading, with his implications about the amateurishness of Packard.

Mallon grimaced, frowning down at the coffee table, picking his words with care. Or at least giving that impression. "Naturally," he said slowly, not looking at me, "I would prefer you to stop, but I don't at all expect you to stop, at least not right away. So that's why I wanted to talk with you. To be sure you understood one or two things before you met with anybody else."

"One thing I don't understand," I said, "is why you'd prefer me to stop."

"Because you're reopening an unfortunate and ambiguous and potentially dangerous situation that I'd thought was happily closed."

"You don't care who murdered Doug Walford?"

He shrugged, looking at me with an open expression. "I *know* who murdered Doug Walford," he said. "Who paid for it, anyway."

"Frank Althorn."

Another shrug. He drank Tab, put the glass down, and looked at me with his clear eyes, waiting.

I said, "Doug was an employee of yours. I thought there was some sort of code in the private-detective business, you don't rest when one of your own is killed, something like that."

His grin this time was almost pitying; certainly, patronizing. "Well, Mr. Holt," he said, "these days we have insurance, survivors' benefits, retirement programs. And the fact of the matter is, Douglas Walford was not acting as an employee of this company when he got himself into trouble."

"Wasn't he doing work on the Miriam Althorn divorce?"

"In connection with community property only." He held up a hand, for emphasis. "Many of our clients," he said, "perhaps a majority, have diverse business dealings of some sensitivity and secrecy, having nothing to do with the matter on which they've hired us. They like to believe, and I set myself to *make* them believe, that we at Harvey Mallon Security Services are unfailingly discreet and, where necessary, that we wear blinders. When Douglas Walford learned whatever it was he learned that brought all that trouble down on himself, Mr. Holt, he was *not under my instructions.*" His voice rising, he said, "In the truest sense, Walford wasn't working for me at that point at all. That's the fact I want you to understand and take away with you and—" He stopped and took a deep breath, having let some passion or urgency creep out into the open where it could be seen. Then he went on: ". . . and pass on, tell, repeat, to anyone else you discuss this matter with."

"Like Frank Althorn?"

Calm again, he grinned and shook his head, saying, "I doubt you'll ever be in the same room with Frank Althorn, but yes, if you are."

"He's in New York, isn't he?"

"Actually, I believe he's spending most of his time these days in Atlantic City at his hotel."

"His hotel?"

Mallon looked at me as though I was being naughty. "You want me to do your work for you? For free?"

"No, I don't," I said. "Let me think. An Atlantic City hotel would be with a casino, so it's one he's fronting for his mob friends since Althorn is officially clean. And if he's spending most of his time there, it must be new, a new toy, and he's still enjoying it. So it's the most recent casino hotel to open in Atlantic City."

Mallon laughed. "Packard couldn't have done it better himself. Maybe I should hire you."

"We'd have to discuss the survivors' benefits," I told

him. "Would you happen to know which is the newest casino in Atlantic City? Or would that be asking you to work for free?"

"Not a bit," he said, broadly beaming, amused with me. "It's called Neptune's Realm. But I rather like you, Mr. Holt, and I can never resist a play on words, so let me give you a word of advice. When you go to Neptune's Realm, try not to get in over your head."

29

It's been a long while since I made my own meals. In the old days I fed myself with no trouble, but somewhere along the line I lost the skill for it. These days, Robinson does the cooking at home, a job he's good at because he enjoys it. In the kitchen he's master of his domain, director and star and entire cast, and if from time to time he improves upon the script—that is, the recipe—there's no one to complain. Certainly not me. Robinson may not be among the world's great chefs, but within his sphere he's very good.

And it *is* his kitchen, dammit, not mine. Back from Harvey Mallon, with the limousine scheduled to return at two, I wandered around the kitchen trying to put together a simple lunch and realized I had no idea where Robinson keeps things. What would I do if he left me forever for that goddamn series? The search for the right pot, the right knife, the right spoon, finally wore me out and I just gave up and phoned a deli over on 6th Avenue. Among sandwiches, the turkey and cheese and tomato and lettuce with Russian dressing on a roll was the simplest they could offer; I ordered one, and allowed as how I could make my own coffee, thank you.

With the phone in front of me anyway, I called Brett at the number he'd given my service and an irritable young woman answered. I was really interrupting her day, but she went off and got Brett, who sounded his usual cheery self when he came on the line, saying, "Welcome back. You gonna stick around?"

"Awhile."

"What are you doing this afternoon? Want to come watch Maria shoot aprons?"

Shoot aprons? With a camera, presumably. "Sure," I said, and he gave me the address, and I told him I'd be over in midafternoon sometime. Then, reluctantly, I took that list out of my pocket and spread it on the chest-high butcher-block island in the middle of the kitchen. Everything in this room was clean and neat, except where I'd made small disturbances in search of utensils, and now this list was in the middle of it, spoiling things. The piece of paper had creases and wrinkles now, from my pocket, angling across the hand-written names.

It was strange how the existence of that list depersonalized the people involved. As nothing more than one of a group of names, "Anita Imperato" meant almost as little as "Vera Slote," and "Terry Young" was as anonymous as "Helen Mayhew." Well, it was time to bring those names back to life, wasn't it? Always bearing in mind Bly's phrasing of the question: Which nine of these people had *not* betrayed my friendship? Remembering that, I started phoning them, and had made dates with three when the doorbell announced the arrival of my sandwich.

The kid recognized me, and wanted my autograph, which I gave him on a piece of my memo paper, then went back down to the kitchen and transferred the huge sloppy sandwich to a plate. Eating it with knife and fork, washing it down with San Pellegrino, I made more phone calls, and by the time the limo came back at two I had a dinner date with Terry and Gretchen Young for tonight, a meeting with my lawyer, Morton Adler, at ten tomorrow morning, and dinner with Jerry and Nora Henderson tomorrow evening. Ann Goodman (who'd found that locked bathroom door concealing Doug's body) was not in her office at CBS News, and I didn't know her social-worker friend Helen Mayhew well enough to try calling her direct. Which left Bill Ackerson's date of that evening, the fashion designer Vera Slote, whose business address was on West 36th Street, in the garment district. Rather than call her, a person I didn't really know, I decided to stop by her office; it might be helpful to see the office, too. So I gave that address to Ralph the driver, and off we went, uptown.

Which would I hate more, doing all this or not doing it? I'd soon find out.

30

Vera Slote ran no small operation. The large gray-stone building in midblock on 36th Street was full of nine floors of garment-industry tenants, among whom she was apparently the most important, with two floors listed on the building directory next to the elevator: "5   Vera Slote, Inc. Deliveries. 6 Vera Slote, Inc. Offices. Showrooms." No other tenant on either floor. I entered the battered-looking elevator and pushed "6."

Ms. Slote wasted little concern on the style of her reception area. The elevator opened to a small room painted battleship gray, with a black floor and white ceiling. A gray leather sofa was the only furnishing, but the walls sported large color photos of a striking-looking model posed—in Vera Slote designs, no doubt—on a fashion-show runway.

Opposite the elevator was a gray metal door beside a receptionist's window partly covered by a sheet of Lucite. I went over and looked through and was surprised to see a motherly sort of woman in there, doing needlepoint. Then I saw that the needlepoint square, which she'd almost finished, featured red letters on a black field, reading "FUCK, NO." She looked back at me and smiled and said, "You're Sam Holt."

I wanted to say "fuck, no," I really did, more than almost anything, but I resisted the temptation. "To see Vera Slote, please," I said.

"I'll buzz her assistant."

"Well, it's Miss Slote I want to see."

The receptionist had already punched out some numbers on her phone console. "You'll have to go to Paris for that," she told me, and said into the phone, "Darlene, Sam Holt is here. You know, the TV star. Asking for Vera. Right." Hanging up, she told me, "Ms. Rabinowitz will be right out."

"Thank you," I said, and spent the time studying the fashion pictures on the walls. The model, the same one in all the pictures, was very tall and thin, with a strong-featured face, heavy-lidded eyes, and black hair in a tight helmet style, the ends curving up under her ears. She would have distracted from designs any less dramatic than those Vera Slote had put on her.

The metal door opened, and a short skinny young woman with sharp features but a bright smile came out and extended a long thin hand for me to shake. Her clothing, being at the cutting edge of fashion, looked absurd but important. "A pleasure to meet you," she told me. "I'm Darlene Rabinowitz, your biggest fan."

"Thank you," I said, with a big smile.

"*And* modest," she said, approving of me. I gave her back her hand, and she said, "Vera's in Paris. Can I help in any way?"

"It's a private matter," I said. "She was at a party at my house last month."

"Was she really? Keeping you to herself, eh?" Darlene Rabinowitz's smile now seemed carnivorous.

"She was there with a friend of mine," I explained. "Her doctor, I think. Bill Ackerson." Seeing the blank look on her face, I said, "The point is, I'd like to talk to Vera as soon as I could."

"Well, she's due back . . ." She frowned, and glanced toward the motherly receptionist (who was back at her needle-point) as though for help. Instead of asking anything, though, she shook her head and looked back at me, and said, "It's all up in the air, really. If things go . . . She might be there a week or two, or if the deal falls apart, she could be on a plane right now. Certainly be back by the end of the month, probably earlier."

"If she'd phone me . . ." I got out one of my cards, which has my name but Zack Novak's address and phone, and on it I wrote my New York number. "Tell her it's about the party she was at."

"I sure will," she promised, and flashed that smile again. "And if there's anything *I* can do—"

"Thanks a lot," I said, and pushed the button for the elevator.

"Edna here knows how to get in touch with me," she said, with a gesture at the needlepointing receptionist.

"I'll remember that."

Darlene Rabinowitz stood smiling at me until the elevator arrived. I smiled back, and when I had stepped aboard and the closing door had shut her off, I relaxed my aching facial muscles. Alone in the elevator, I could grimace and yawn and stretch my jaw.

Vera Slote. A very successful designer, from the look of things. A large elaborate business without a lot of out-front display. Was that a cover for a hired killer?

And my next suspect, to go from the ridiculous to the just as ridiculous, was Brett Burgess's girlfriend, Maria Kaiser.

31

Maria Kaiser, a professional photographer, a free-lance who works mostly for *Gourmet* and other up-scale magazines, is a bubbly girl with a spine of steel, the fit and right companion for Brett Burgess, which scares them both. Neither wants to be tied down, neither wants to lose freedom, but when they're away from each other, both are miserable.

We met today at three-thirty in a loft building on West 31st Street, fourth floor. A wide high-ceilinged place with white walls, it was almost completely open from large front windows through to large back windows, the space broken only by frequent fat round pillars painted white. The floor was light oak, highly polished, and the ceiling, crisscrossed with pipes and structural beams, all also painted white. Halfway down the left wall, an enclosed section contained the stairwell, elevator shaft, toilet, office, kitchen, and storeroom.

This loft was a space for rent, by the hour or by the day, for whatever commercial use you had in mind. Videos had been taped here, fashion lines had been introduced to the

155

press here, book publication parties had been held here, and today Maria Kaiser was here on an advertising assignment, shooting a new line of chic kitchenwear for an ad spread in *Fashions of the Times*. Aprons, as Brett had said, but also peignoirs, hostess gowns, things like that, the client taking the broad view and including whatever you might wear *to* the kitchen, as well as in it.

In both still photography and film, the longest preparation time is always spent with the lights, which remained true today. Three lighting men were busily at work when I arrived, barking at one another, moving reflectors an inch this way or that, adding or removing "barn doors," those flat black sheets of metal angled in front of each light to let only so much illumination reach the subject. Meanwhile, a dozen other people, from the ad agency or the manufacturer, wandered around and waited.

Brett and Maria were at a card table by the rear windows, seated on plain metal chairs and drinking coffee out of Styrofoam. I got my own coffee from the tall metal urn in the kitchen, my own chair from the stack in the corner, and joined them.

Maria at work is a very different person from the cheerful enthusiast I usually know. Her manner becomes tense, absorbed, almost fretful, as though she had some premonition of disaster. Vertical frown lines appear between her brows, she raps tabletops with her fingernails, and when spoken to, she mutters or gives short answers or glowers as though angry to be interrupted.

Brett, who is happy and expansive and self-confident when at work, never knows how to deal with Maria the perfectionist, and frequently makes the mistake of trying to jolly her out of it. When I joined them with my chair and coffee, she gave me a quick distracted half smile and went back to frowning at the light crew, while Brett flashed in my direction his sunniest smile and with false heartiness said, "We're going to be in Italy in October!"

"We are?"

"Maria and me."

"That's nice," I said.

"Not exactly together," he said, "but we'll work it out, won't we, babe?"

"Mm," she said, and looked at her watch.

"Tell me about it, Brett," I said, mostly to make him leave her alone.

So he told me about it, while Maria fretted and twitched beside him and the lighting men shouted at one another about hot spots and dead spots, opening and closing their barn doors. In October and November, Brett would be in Rome, working on a TV miniseries, while for two weeks in October Maria would be in the south of Italy, working out of Naples, on assignment for *Travel & Leisure*. They would be a couple of hundred miles apart, but surely they'd be able to get together a few times, and Brett had been unwise enough to try to talk to Maria *now* about the arrangements they could make, a conversation he was happy to continue with me, but without her.

Then at last the lighting men pronounced themselves satisfied, and Maria went over to confer with some other people before actually starting the shoot. An ad-agency man was methodically taking Polaroid shots, in order to see what her pictures were going to look like, a fairly common and completely ridiculous practice that Maria bears with the polite restraint of the thoroughbred.

The instant she had left the table, Brett stopped talking about Italy and started talking about me: "What's up, Sam? Why the jumping around, all of a sudden leaving New York and then all of a sudden coming back?"

"It's about Doug Walford," I said.

At first, he drew a blank on the name. "Who?"

"My friend who was—"

"Oh, my God! The guy who killed himself! Leinster, wasn't it?"

"He was calling himself that. But his name was Walford, and he didn't kill himself."

He nodded. "You made a big point about that at the inquest. But it couldn't be anything else, right? The guy was depressed. Listen, it happens."

I know actors have a reputation for stupidity, and though I'm one myself, I want to present a defense right here. What may sometimes look like thickness or dumbness isn't that at all, but is simply the result of the way the actor's mind is disciplined. I know Brett to be a very bright guy, but there are times when he can seem awfully obtuse, and that's the reason why.

The point is, actors are the only people I know of who are trained to think in terms of *character* rather than *story.* A chemist, an airline pilot, a waiter in a restaurant—every one of them is used to being interested in the sequence of events, what happens next. Only the actor has developed himself to think about *who* rather than *what,* and that's why Brett, of all the people at the party, was the likeliest to still think of Doug as Doug Leinster, the character name under which he'd first been introduced. And it's also why, once the character had been written out of the story by the inquest, Brett was the most likely to lose all curiosity about him.

I suppose what saves me from this occupational hazard, to the extent that I am saved, is the two other occupations I've dabbled in. Both the cop and the writer are very involved in story, in the sequence of events, and both are also interested— as the actor is but as, say, your Laundromat gossip is not—in individual personality. Remembering this, I said, "Brett, I knew the guy, and suicide wouldn't be his way. It just wasn't like him; it was out of character."

"If you say so," he said, nodding, accepting that. "But so what?"

How could I answer that question? I looked over at Maria, beside the set. Everything had been adjusted to her satisfaction now, and for the first time she was peering through the camera, tilted downward on its tall tripod as though surprised. She would have been out of character, too, if she were the one who'd followed Doug upstairs, moved quickly close to him in the hall, jabbed the hypodermic needle into his arm or his back as he opened the bathroom door, bundled him into that room already falling, shut the door with one last look over her shoulder to be sure she was alone, and set the scene for suicide.

Completely out of character. Only the quick competence sounded like Maria, that and the setting of the scene, as she had set the scene this afternoon for photography. But the rest? Why should anybody who was so good with a camera ever reach for a nastier tool?

But *someone* had been out of character that night. If not Maria, who? I only knew it hadn't been Doug.

32

Maria's shoot was finished a little after five. "Just ten minutes into overtime," as she said later, laughing, much more relaxed with the job done and her black leather camera bag full of exposed rolls of film in little black plastic tubes.

Like the tube containing the pills that were supposed to have killed Doug.

Maria has a small place on East 17th Street, which Brett shares with her when in the city. They accepted my offer of a ride downtown, and in the nestlike comfort of the limo it was at last possible to talk about the party, though I was reluctant to spoil Maria's good mood. She and Brett sat hand in hand on the rear seat while I faced them, my elbow on the TV-refrigerator console, and for the first five minutes or so they rattled on happily together about their overlapping Italian trips. At a pause in the conversation, I said, "I told Brett why I came back to the city."

"Because you love it here," she said.

"More than that."

161

Brett said, "It's something to do with that friend of his that died at the party."

Maria frowned. "The man who committed suicide?"

"Sam says he didn't."

"He didn't," I agreed. "So what I'm trying to do, Maria, is figure out where everybody was during that last ten minutes before we found his body."

Maria looked at me as though I were out of focus and it wasn't her fault. "Where everybody was?" she echoed. "Why?"

"Because Doug was murdered," I told her.

She gave a tentative grin, holding on for the punch line. I didn't have one, so I just sat there and waited for her to absorb it. After a while, she frowned at Brett, who shrugged and raised his brows and said, "That's what he says, honey."

"That's silly." She looked at me again, a levelheaded level-eyed girl used to looking at reality through a camera and seeing when the details were wrong. "That's crazy," she told me. "It's . . . Packard."

I had to laugh. "I know it is. 'Where were you at such and such a time?' Absolutely Packard."

"And you're serious."

"Sorry, Maria, yes."

"Hmm," she said, frowning just with the left side of her mouth, trying to remember. "Where was I when your friend was murdered."

"When he was found," I corrected. "When you heard he was dead."

"Hmm. Sam, that was *weeks* ago."

"I know, I know."

"Let me see," she said. "That was . . . Well, of course, I heard the water running, too, but I didn't think anything about it."

"The water?"

"In the bathroom. I went upstairs and the door was locked and the water was running, so there was somebody in there, so I went on up to your room—I figured you wouldn't mind."

"Wait a minute," I said. "You mean, you tried that bathroom door before Ann Goodman did?"

"I must have," she said. "She was on the way upstairs when I was on the way down."

"And was there anybody else up there? Did you see anybody else?"

Slowly she shook her head. "Just there was somebody moving around in the second-floor bathroom, and—"

"Moving around?"

"Moving a glass or something, I don't know. And the water was running."

"So Doug was in there already." And, I didn't say it out loud, the killer was probably in there, too, setting the scene.

"I guess he was," Maria said. "So I went on up to the third floor. And passed Ann Goodman on my way back down."

"Okay. Who were you with before you went upstairs?"

"Oh, Lord, I don't know," she said. "The party went on for *hours,* Sam."

"Well, were you still coming downstairs when Ann said there was something wrong? Were you still on the stairs?"

"No, I was . . ." We were stopped at a traffic light, a garish orange truck next to us, reflecting light that tinged us all faintly rose. Maria frowned at that orange wall as though trying to figure out how to soften it for the camera. Then we started forward, the truck turned onto the side street away from us, and Maria's brow cleared. "Terry Young," she said. "I went back to talk to Terry."

"Back?"

"Yes." She looked at me with some surprise. "I *am* remembering. I didn't think I would."

"You were talking to Terry before you went upstairs," I suggested. And I remembered Anita saying she'd been on line at the bar behind Terry just before the discovery of Doug's body, so that tied together: Maria and Terry talking, Terry getting a drink while Maria goes upstairs to the bathroom, Terry and Maria talking again when she came back down.

"Yes," she said. "Terry and . . . There was a group of us."

"Do you remember who?"

"We were talking about . . . pictures. Cameras."

Brett laughed. "A busman's holiday."

"Kind of," she agreed, taking it seriously. "We all had different relationships with the camera, uses of the camera. Terry and the newspaper, and the camera just . . . What did he say? It *verifies* the facts."

"And who else?"

"That very dramatic designer woman that Bill Ackerson brought."

"Vera Slote."

"Yes. She has her own staff photographer, she does everything in-house, the camera's very important to her, too. Oh, I remember! Jerry Henderson."

"That makes sense," I said. Jerry Henderson is a director; the movie camera is his tool just as the still camera is Maria's.

"It was the four of us," Maria said. "Jerry and Terry and Vera Slote and me. And then the group broke up, and when I came back downstairs, I just talked with Terry for a while."

And Jerry Henderson, according to Anita, had gone over to talk with his wife, Nora, which had led Anita to the bar. "That's fine, Maria," I said. "Thanks a lot."

The memory chore finished, Maria naturally went on to the reason for it all, saying, "You're trying to figure out where everybody was, because the person who wasn't anywhere is the killer."

"That's right."

"Opportunity." She considered that, then looked at me again, saying, "*I* had the opportunity."

"When you went upstairs, you mean."

"If your friend was killed . . . What was the murder weapon?"

"Hypodermic needle."

"Oh, well, that's easy. I could have done that."

I was aware of Brett looking from Maria to me and back again. I said nothing.

Maria followed her own thought: "I could have left Terry—"

"The group."

"No, just Terry by then. I could have gone upstairs and done it, whatever it was, and then come back down, saw Ann Goodman, talked with Terry again, told anybody who asked that I went all the way up to the third floor."

"I don't believe you did," I said.

"But I could have." Maria had very, very level eyes when she wanted to.

"You could have," I admitted.

"What about Brett?" she asked. "Does he have an alibi?"

"He was with me," I said, "the whole time."

She laughed. "*That* was my mistake! I should have been talking to the host."

"It would make it easier."

We were nearing their neighborhood, and Brett was frowning now like a thundercloud. He reached over and picked up Maria's leather camera bag. We both watched him unzip it and reach in and pull out one of the black plastic film tubes with its gray plastic cap. He hefted it in his hand. He looked at me, and I knew we were both remembering the tube just like that lying on the bathroom floor, capsules artfully spread out from it. The black cornucopia. Brett said, slowly, "You want to be careful, Sam."

"I know it."

"You don't want to break anything, Sam."

"I'll try my best not to, Brett."

"Sam's trying to find out the truth, that's all," Maria told him.

"I know what Sam's doing." We watched him put the film tube back in the bag, zip the compartment shut.

Conversation limped on for the next few minutes, until we stopped in front of Maria's address. They got out, thanking me for the lift, Maria being a little brighter than necessary, Brett being very reserved.

"See you soon," I said.

"Sure," Maria said.

"Mm," Brett said.

33

Neptune's Realm had a New York tie-line phone; I dialed it and asked who was appearing in the main room right now. "No show Mondaytuesdaywednesday, sir," I was told.

"Okay," I said. "Who's appearing Thursdayfridaysaturday?"

"This coming weekend, sir?"

"Yes, please," I said, with an edge in my voice. I was in a bad mood because of Brett—because I basically agreed with Brett—and it was hard to keep it under control.

"In the Ocean Theater this weekend," the Jersey-accented voice told me, "Neptune's Realm is proud to present the return engagement of the Queen of Comedy, Sandy Sheriff, appearing with the fine Broadway and recording singing star Garry Dwyer."

I'd been hoping it would be somebody I already knew, but that was all right. "Thank you," I said.

"May we assist you with reservations?"

"No, thank you."

It was just six o'clock, and I was home again in my empty house on 10th Street, edgy and guilty and not at all sure I was doing the right thing. It was three o'clock on the Coast. Where would Bly be? At the studio, probably, with her pilot, and I shouldn't phone her there when I didn't really have anything to say. So I called her at home instead, on the off chance she was there, and got the answering machine. It was good to hear her voice. I left no message.

I was seated at the desk in my office, and when I hung up from that call, I turned and frowned at myself in the same amber-tinted mirror I'd looked in when Doug had first phoned me, calling himself Holton Hickey. "By God, Holt," I told my reflection, referring to myself as Doug would have, "you sure are feeling sorry for yourself, aren't you? Let's cure that."

So I cured it. I got up from the desk and left the office and went across the hall to stand in the bathroom doorway, looking at the place where Doug Walford's dead or dying body had been so carefully, artistically, theatrically arranged. The capsules had been fanned out on the floor here, the film tube on its side there, his legs stretched out there and there, dead hands hanging down between his thighs. Head lolling there, eyes filmy gray. Okay, Holt? Okay.

Cured, I went back to the office, sat at my desk again, and reached for the phone.

Harvey Mallon, as I'd suspected, was a workaholic, still in the office after 6 P.M. on a lovely June day. I was put right through to him, and that sugar-honey voice said, "Thought of another question since this morning, Mr. Holt?"

"Just one," I said. "Would you take me on as a client?"

"Good God, no," he said, sounding surprised. "You mean, to chase after Frank Althorn? Certainly not."

"I don't mean that," I said. "I have a list of ten names. I'd like simple backgrounders, that's all."

"Looking for what?"

"A handle. A pressure point for mobsters or whoever."

"Oh oh oh oh," he said. "This is your suspect list. Which of them could the mob get to, force to do their dirty work, is that it?"

"That's it."

"Why in God's name are you so naïve, Mr. Holt, if you'll forgive me, as to offer to give me those names? Think of the people I could sell you out to."

"Mr. Mallon," I said, "if *you'll* forgive *me*, you're the most frightened man I've ever met. You won't doublecross me, you won't doublecross anyone, for the same reason you won't risk yourself to help anyone. You clutch your success, you watch your ass at all times. If you say you'll take the job, you'll probably overcharge me, but you'll deliver and you won't fool around. It's the pact you've made with God."

"You can go straight to hell, Mr. Holt," he said. "It's no deal."

"Just a second," I said. "If you *won't* take the job, I have to tell you, I'm not as trustworthy as you are."

That kept him on the line, in more ways than one. "Meaning what?"

"I'll be seeing Frank Althorn this weekend."

"You will not."

"I will. I have my methods, Watson. And the question is, what would you like me to say to Frank Althorn about Harvey Mallon?"

"You dirty rotten son of a bitch," he said.

I laughed at him. "That isn't what you'd like me to say."

I remembered the ice tongs and the Tab, I remembered the name-dropping and the plush quiet office and the copy of *Soldier of Fortune* magazine on the coffee table and the smooth pleasure in having clients whose dangerous secrets are safe around Harvey Mallon. I remembered the drunk driver who bought the cop who'd controlled him.

"You filthy prick," Mallon said. "You disgusting piece of shit."

I let him go on like that, till he wore himself out, and then I said, "The other reason you're the one I want to hire is that I know you're conscientious, and you'll do a good job."

The astonished silence caused by that remark was followed by a sudden bark of laughter. "By God, Holt," he said, "you're better than you were on television!"

"Thank you."

"If you ever need a job, or you're bored, what a wonderful coldhearted street agent you'd make!"

"You trying to hire me?" Like Doug, again.

"I would, by God. How deep a background you want on these people?"

"First pressing only. Criminal records, business associations, immediate family, employment history, that sort of thing."

"A thousand dollars a name."

"Delivered to me in New York Monday morning."

"Today is Tuesday? Fine."

I gave him the ten names, with addresses, then said, "Send the bill to my accountant, Untenberg and Platt, 13636 Ventura Boulevard, Sherman Oaks, California, 91423."

"Fine," he said, and then, "you know, Mr. Holt, I hope you *do* keep poking around in this mess. I hope you learn everything you want and see everybody you want and do everything you want. I hope you become just as much trouble to those people as your friend Douglas Walford was."

"Thanks," I said, but he'd already hung up, so I called Karen Platt out in Sherman Oaks to tell her Mallon's bill would be coming in and should be paid, and then I called my industrious agent, Zack Novak, and said, "Who do we know who knows Sandy Sheriff?"

"The comedian? You have a property? Sam, I'm not sure that's a good pairing. I don't think I see you and that woman working too—"

"You don't see me working at all, Zack," I pointed out. "But it isn't that."

"Sam," he said, "I'm doing my best for you, and why wouldn't I? What's the commission on no employment?"

"Okay, Zack, I know. But I want an intro to Sandy Sheriff because she can introduce me to somebody else."

"Am I supposed to follow all this?" he asked me.

"No."

"That's all right, then. Sandy Sheriff's manager is Garson/Modell; we've got three clients over there. What do you need?"

"She's playing Neptune's Realm in Atlantic City this weekend. The owner is Frank Althorn. I want to meet Frank Althorn, socially, casually."

"You think the owner hangs around with the help?"

"He's spending his time at the hotel," I explained, "because it's his new toy. I think he'll drop in to giggle with the celebrity he hired for the big room, yes, I do. You say she's managed by Garson/Modell. Who opens for her on the road, do you know?"

"No, but I can find out."

"If it's a guy named Robin Corrigan, I know him. He used to shepherd me, back when I had a career."

"Don't twist the knife, Sam, okay?"

"Not twisting, Zack," I assured him. "Just jiggling it a little."

"Did you hear the Burt Reynolds line?" he asked me.

"Which Burt Reynolds line?"

" 'I'm a star over fifty-five miles an hour.' "

"Zack, I do know other people have the same problem," I told him. "I know people go to see Columbo and walk away from Peter Falk. I know Farrah Fawcett couldn't get arrested for six years. Okay, when Reynolds gets out of the car and puts on a tie, the movie doesn't make money, but he's *working*, Zack. I wouldn't mind being in a bomb if at least I was employed."

"Do me a favor, Sam," he said. "Never say that to a producer."

"You get me into a conversation with a producer, Zack, I'll know what to say."

"That's nice. I'll get back to you on the Sandy Sheriff thing."

"Thanks, Zack," I said, and hung up, and thought awhile about the time when I too was managed by Garson/Modell. Stars in ongoing series are encouraged to do a lot of personal appearances, for which they are quite decently paid, and the details of such appearances are handled by management companies like Garson/Modell. An employee of theirs named Robin Corrigan used to go with me every time I did an autographing session at a shopping center or gave a talk to a police chief's convention or whatever the appearance happened to be. Robin's title was road manager, and his job was to see that the lodging was adequate, the money was paid, the circumstances were as outlined in the contract. If anything made me unhappy, I was to tell Robin, and he'd take care of it, and for this service Garson/Modell took fifteen percent of my appearance fees, and they were well worth it.

For somebody like Sandy Sheriff the services of a Robin Corrigan were even more necessary. In the jargon of the business, he would open her and close her. That is, in something like this four-day appearance at Neptune's Realm, the road manager would come to the hotel either with the star or just ahead of her, examine the accommodations, check the special requirements in the contract (for overnights, I always used to insist on San Pellegrino in the suite), deal with the main room's stage manager and the orchestra leader and whoever else might be important or useful, and generally smooth the path. Once the star was ensconced and satisfied, the road manager would leave, possibly to service other clients, not returning until the final day of the engagement, when he'd collect the salary, pay the bills, distribute the tips, and unruffle whatever feathers had been ruffled in the interim.

If I have to be honest, it isn't merely the work I miss these days, it's also that sense of importance you get from being at the center of an ongoing activity. All I had to do back then was cock an eyebrow at Robin Corrigan, and whatever the problem was *he would take care of it*. There was something wonderful about it all, no matter how false and ephemeral it was, and the truth is, I liked it.

I was still thinking about all this, remembering a few particular moments when Robin had been outrageously tough on my behalf, and I may even have been smiling a bit in reminiscence, when the phone rang. Assuming it was Zack with an answer to my question, I picked up and it was Bill Ackerson, saying, "How's it going, pal?"

"Well, it's going," I said. "How's my favorite sawbones?"

"Just as wonderful as ever. Sam, I've been thinking all day about our dinner conversation last night."

"Doug, you mean."

"What else? Listen, Sam, I volunteered last night to do what I could to help, and I want you to know I meant it then, and I still mean it now."

"Thanks. I know you mean it."

"I could be—I don't know—I could be a sounding board. You've got theories, suspicions, problems, confusions, you can talk them all out with *me*. I'm close to the situation, but I'm not involved."

"Expanding into psychiatry, Bill?"

He laughed, and said, "No, forensic medicine. Lunchtime today I looked at the show with the hypodermic murder."

"You mean the PACKARD?"

"Right. 'A Game That Two Can Play,' it was called."

"That's right, I remember that."

He said, "I didn't have time to watch the whole show, so I fast-forwarded to the murder scene and the explanation, and you know, Sam, I think you're right."

"That Doug was killed that way? I know I'm right. Bill, how do you happen to have a tape of that show?"

"I have them all, man. I'm a fan, didn't you know that?"

"But Jesus, Bill," I said, "you have five *years* of PACKARD?"

"Any time you want to run through your history, just let me know."

"I don't believe this," I said. "Bill, you never cease to amaze me."

"I never mentioned it," he said, " 'cause it sounded kinda Mickey Mouse, you know? But it's true. I'm a fan, so I got all the shows. You have your own cabinet in the den."

"You couldn't have taped every one of those off the air."

"Most, I did, either first time or in rerun. And remember Robin Corrigan?"

"This is a ridiculous coincidence," I said. "I was just thinking about Robin."

"I got to know him when you got ptomaine that time, and he helped me get the tapes I didn't have. Listen, Sam, now that I've come out of the closet on this . . ." And he hesitated.

What on earth was coming next? I said, "What, Bill? What is it?"

"The seven shows you wrote," he said. "If I bring them around, would you autograph them?"

"Autograph the *cassettes?*"

"Yeah. Why not?"

I couldn't think why not. *We are at the cutting edge of fandom,* I thought. "Okay, Bill," I said.

"How about tonight? You wanna do dinner again?"

"No, actually I'm having dinner with Terry and Gretchen Young tonight."

"They're suspects."

"Bill, I hate that part of it."

So we talked about that a little, what I'd done so far on the Doug problem and what I'd set up for the future. He volunteered to call Vera Slote in Paris and ask her my where-were-you-when question, but I said I'd rather wait till she got back and I could talk to her in person. He said, *"That's* when we'll do dinner."

"Fine."

"Keep in touch. Give me something to do on this thing."

I promised I would, and hung up, and when the phone rang again five minutes later, it still wasn't Zack, but it was better than Zack: It was Robin Corrigan. "Hey, baby," said the well-remembered easygoing voice. "What can I do for you?"

"You open for Sandy Sheriff these days?"

"A lovely lady, Sam," he said. "I shit you not, a lovely, lovely lady."

"That's nice," I said. "Do you suppose she could casually, as though it wasn't planned, introduce me to Frank Althorn this weekend?"

"You got it," he said. "Between shows Thursday night, you'll come down as Sandy's guest."

"Terrific."

"You'll be in the audience the first show; she'll introduce you from the stage. All you have to do is stand up and smile and sit down."

"I remember how to do that."

"You're a very quick study, Sam. I've always said so. Then you come around to the dressing room after. Frank's already invited himself back for drinks. It won't be a mob— eight or ten people. You want him to finance a movie?"

"Not exactly."

"Why not? You could be his Pia Zadora."

I laughed, happy to hear this outrageous man's voice again. "I'll see you Thursday," I said.

"San Pellegrino in the suite, right?"

"Robin," I said, "if I ever decide to get married, you're on the short list."

34

Terry and Gretchen Young live with their three children in the Midwood section of Brooklyn, just east of Flatbush Avenue, a neighborhood of sprawling one-family houses on large lots, just a few blocks from big chunky apartment buildings. There was a tricycle on the front porch, and a tire swing in the back yard, and it was all as far from Terry's often squalid work life on the *News* as it's possible to get, which was probably the idea.

I had Anita with me, and we were using another drive-it-yourself Mercury from the car-rental place. We arrived at seven-thirty, shortly before sundown, to find another couple there, named Bob and Kitty Marchwood, so with them and the kids and my natural reluctance to raise the subject at all, we didn't get around to the question of Doug and the party for a long, long time.

Terry explained to me once that the reason Gretchen looks Irish is because there are deep links between the Teutons and the Celts, way back in the mists of time. "Those northern swamps," he told me, "all across that chopped-up top of Europe there—they all produced the same people, straight across from Ireland over as far as Finland. Pale skin, pale hair, pale eyes. Winter without sun gives them that gloom, summer without night gives them that recklessness, the cold makes them brave and suspicious." On the other hand, I think Terry thinks Gretchen looks Irish because he's in love with her.

In fact, Gretchen is completely German, having been born thirty-some years ago in the other Frankfurt, the one in East Germany. When she was four, her parents escaped to West Berlin with their three children, and that's where Gretchen grew up, learning English in school and then attending Berlin Free University, majoring in Romance languages. Work as an interpreter between French and German led her eventually to a job with Interpol, which after a while brought her to New York due to some minor ramification of the drug organization that became known as the French Connection. That was when Terry met her and decided life would not be possible without her.

Apparently, it was very romantic. Gretchen was happy with her work and her independence and didn't see any real need to hook herself up with some overweight New York reporter. Terry pursued his northern blond beauty to Paris, and then to Berlin, where her father became his most fervent partisan. Terry told me once that Gretchen's father would sometimes say to her, in Terry's presence, "You got to marry this man; he's just like me." Terry laughed and said, "A pre-Freudian household is a wonderful thing, Sam."

Anyway, they married. Gretchen did some script translating for foreign films, got on the waiting list for a translator's job at the UN, and then started having children. Somewhere along the line she metamorphosed, and gradually became the complete hausfrau: a little heavy, a compulsive housekeeper, a good cook and terrific baker, a deeply involved mother. I'd always assumed she was content with the metamorphosis, but something she said at the Doug party made me wonder. I'd been complaining again about not being able to find any acting work—I probably complain about that too much, come to think of it—and Gretchen said, "Like me, I guess. Our glory days are over." It was early in the party, and more guests were arriving at that moment, so I never had a chance to follow through on that statement, but was that what she actually believed? Were her glory days over?

Good God, are mine?

Anyway, the only thing German about Gretchen's cooking is the lavish quantities she serves. Otherwise, for company, she does the normal things with chicken breasts or veal. The other couple present, the Marchwoods, were neighborhood people that Terry and Gretchen knew through their children, Bob Marchwood being something in the public-relations department of Metropolitan Life Insurance Company, a job that gave him a theoretical link both to Terry's newspaper work and my background in show biz. The link was a strained one, but it survived chitchat before, during, and after dinner. (At the beginning of the evening, the rest of us all had to resolutely ignore the fact that Kitty Marchwood was being dazzled by the presence of a celebrity—me—but she soon got over it when I proved to be neither as interesting as she might have hoped nor as terrible as she might have feared.)

At nine-thirty, both Marchwoods began using the word "babysitter," which in middle-class circles is a synonym for "good-bye." So they went, with much handshaking all around, leaving the four of us in Gretchen's quite Germanic living room—a high plate rail bearing antique souvenir platters, for instance, and small throw rugs on the highly polished blond wood floor—and after a minute or two of conversation about nothing in particular, Terry said to me, "For somebody

who's supposed to be an actor, you're about as hard to read
as *Dick and Jane*.''

"I am?''

"There's something you've been crazy to get off your
chest all evening.''

Smiling to soften it, Gretchen told me, "Your face when
you saw poor Kitty and Bob! Kitty was quite brought down
by it at first.'' Gretchen doesn't have an accent as such,
merely a more-precise-than-usual way of speaking, combined
with a fluidity of vowels she probably picked up from learning French.

Feeling embarrassed and guilty, I said, "Was I that obvious? Jesus, I didn't want to be rude.''

"No, no, you were your charming self,'' Gretchen assured
me. "Kitty got over it very nearly at once. She loved you
madly when they departed.''

"What Sam wants to talk about,'' Anita said, breaking the
ice with a sledgehammer, "is his friend's death at that party.''

"Doug Walford,'' Terry said, nodding, looking grim. "God,
I wish there was a story in there.''

I didn't get it. "What kind of story?''

"The mob—somebody—reached right into a private house,''
he said, stretching his own arm out in demonstration, closing
his fist on a handful of air and giving it a twist, "right in the
middle of a party, and touched the guy they wanted.''

"You accept that, then,'' I said. "That Doug was
murdered.''

"Well, naturally.'' Terry seemed surprised. "I talked to
him maybe half an hour before, you know?''

"I remember seeing you with him.''

Now Terry patted the air, soothingly. "I didn't break our
agreement, don't worry. I went along with his cover story. I
just wanted a sense of the guy.''

"I knew that's what you were doing.''

"And he was enjoying himself," Terry said. "He liked what he was in."

I frowned. "Are you sure?"

"He was tense, he was in some rough situation, but . . ." Terry glanced over at Gretchen, considered, sipped at his after-dinner beer—the women were having white wine, I was having San Pellegrino—then looked back at me. "There's people like that," he said. "They need to be out on the edge to enjoy life, they need to be in trouble, get that old adrenaline shock. I used to be one of them myself, the hotshot boy reporter. Spend your life passing on the curve."

I remembered Doug's occasional daring when we were together on the force, his description of police work as "chicken-shit," his deciding to accept the job Harvey Mallon offered him. But I said, "He was very tense, Terry." I sensed Anita watching, listening, not saying anything. I said, "He was depressed and troubled."

"All part of the kick," Terry said, and shrugged it away.

"Doug wasn't reckless."

"Sure he was." Terry grinned at me. "He learned some things he shouldn't know about mob business, right?"

"Something like that."

"The *mob* knew he knew. How did they find out?"

"He never told me."

"Only one way," Terry assured me. "From your pal himself. Doug was playing more of a game than you knew about."

Which was probably true. Which was almost certainly true. I remembered that, before Doug had moved in with me, he'd supported himself by robbing liquor stores, a detail I hadn't mentioned to Anita or Terry or anyone else. So he was less than a saint. But he was still, by God, my houseguest when they put him away. I said, "Whatever he was up to, they did kill him. So what do you mean, you wish it was a story?"

"We got the wrong verdict," he said. "Give me a willful murder by party or parties, I've got something I can go to my editor with. We've got a homicide, we've got a celebrity, we've got the sanctity of the home, we've got the faceless mob. . . . Anybody ever figure out how they got in?"

"Walked in," I said, and explained why it had to have been someone invited to the party. Neither Terry nor Gretchen would believe it at first, and Anita added her own two cents to the conversation, and it went on long enough for Gretchen to go to the kitchen for more beer and wine and water. Finally they both accepted the physical impossibility of the murderer having been someone other than a guest at the party, and Terry said, "So that gives you a houseful of suspects, right?"

"Well, I've narrowed it some. Down to ten."

"Who?"

"Well, you three, to begin with," I said, being consciously deadpan, gesturing at him and Gretchen and Anita, "and Maria Kai—"

Terry interrupted me with a whoop of laughter. "You're kidding!"

"Dealing strictly with opportunity," I said.

"Me?" He flung a hand out, gesturing at his wife: *"Gretchen?"*

"Anita," I pointed out, and Anita laughed, without much mirth.

Terry shook his head. "It's a fucking parlor game, Sam."

"Not so loud, Terry," Gretchen told him.

He ignored her. "Colonel Mustard in the library with an unkind word," he said.

"I'm sorry these are unkind words, Terry," I said. "I went away, tried to forget about it, but—"

"All right. All right. I can see you feel foolish about it all."

"I do."

Anita said, "Just before Ann Goodman came downstairs, saying there was somebody in the bathroom and all that, Terry, you and I were over with Robinson at the bar. You were ahead of me on line."

"I was?"

"You don't remember?"

"If you say so, Anita." Terry turned to his wife: "Gretchen, do *you* have any idea where you were when the party was so rudely interrupted?"

"Oh, yes," she said. "It was a very interesting conversation." She pronounced all the syllables in "interesting." "We were a little group who had been together for some time, we were talking about Europe."

"Who was in the group?"

"Well, let me see. There was that very striking designer lady."

"Vera Slote," I said.

"That's right." Gretchen nodded and smiled at me. "She knows Paris very well."

"She's there right now. Who else was with you?"

"Oh, an eclectic group. Well, let me see, Ann Goodman."

"She's the one who came downstairs with the news," I pointed out.

"Yes, that's right, she was before that. And her friend Helen, the social worker—"

"Helen Mayhew."

"Yes." With a lopsided smile, Gretchen said, "Terry tells me they are lesbians. Is that right?"

"I believe so," I said.

"I am so unsophisticated about things like that, I had no idea."

"Well," I said, "I believe they're monogamous. I mean, they wouldn't make passes or anything."

"Oh, no, they're very *respectable*."

"That's right."

"They like to take vacations together in Italy," Gretchen said. "In Tuscany, in small inns."

I said, "So it was you and Vera Slote and Ann and Helen, is that right? Then Ann went away upstairs."

"Well, the lawyer, too," she said. "Your attorney, Morton."

"Morton Adler."

"He wanted to talk about exchange rates," Gretchen said, smiling. Then, looking more serious, she said, "Let me see if I can remember. Morton and I were talking about exchange rates. Then Ann and Helen came over, and the four of us talked for a long time. I *think* it was a long time. Terry came by with his empty glass and said hello—he was getting another drink—and he went away."

"To the bar, with me behind him," Anita said.

"And Vera Slote arrived around that time," Gretchen went on, "and then Ann left, but Helen stayed. I *think* that was the way it went."

"Wait a minute," Terry said. "*I* was talking with Vera Slote."

"About photography," I told him.

Terry looked at me with amused surprise. "Son of a bitch," he said, "you *are* tracking this down, aren't you?"

"That's right."

"All right, who else was I with? Don't tell me, I'll get it."

Gretchen asked us if we'd like anything else to drink, and Anita and I both said no. Anita gave me a sympathetic smile. Meantime, Terry gazed at the ceiling, half taking the problem seriously, half making an elaborate joke out of it. Then he nodded and said, "Brett's girlfriend, Maria, that's who."

"And Jerry Henderson," I told him. "You know, the commercials director."

Terry frowned. "Was he there? Does he say so?"

"I haven't talked to him yet."

Gretchen said, "With two attractive women, Terry won't remember the men."

I said, "The story I get is, Terry and Maria and Vera Slote and Jerry Henderson were a group. Vera and Jerry left, Terry and Maria talked for a minute or two longer, then Maria went upstairs while Terry went to the bar. Terry and Maria were talking again when the party broke up."

"Sounds good," Terry said. "And I guess I said hello to Gretchen on my way to the bar."

"Feeling guilty about talking to all those pretty girls," Gretchen suggested.

"Just comparison shopping," Terry told her comfortably.

Gretchen smiled at me. "A lot goes on at parties."

"Particularly that one," I said.

35

Next morning, when Anita answered the phone, she said, "Sure, he's here. Why not?" Then she rolled over in bed, extending the receiver toward me, saying, "Terry."

I sat up, bunching the pillows to lean on, took the phone, and said, "Good morning."

"So you *do* sleep with your suspects."

"Not all of them," I said. "How are you, Terry?"

"Interested," he said. "You'll find a message on your machine when you get home."

"Saying what?"

"Saying come for a ride."

I laughed. "Sounds ominous."

"That tendency toward melodrama has always hampered your work," he informed me.

Uh-oh. When people joke with that much edge in it, they're very annoyed. So Terry's calm last night hadn't been the whole story. "Okay," I said. "Where do you want me to ride?"

"Out to the Island." Meaning Long Island, in local jargon.
"Why?"

"To meet somebody. I'll tell you more about it on the way."

I had gone out to the Island to meet somebody at the very beginning of all this, and the somebody I'd met that time was now dead and I was mired in this mess. Did I want more of the same? I said, "Terry, no mysteries, all right?"

"You're going to *like* this, dammit," he said. "We're going to talk to somebody about that third biggest question of yours."

Third biggest question? Oh! The question about the third biggest pharmaceutical company. Noticing that Terry too had picked up the paranoia that leads to never saying anything substantive on the telephone, I said, "Where and when?"

"You tell me."

"I have an appointment with my lawyer at ten—"

"Morton Adler."

"Right."

"For how long?"

"Half an hour, maybe a little longer."

"Where?"

"Graybar Building."

"At ten-thirty I'll come to the Lexington Avenue entrance and wait for you."

"But what if I'm late? You can't park around there, Terry."

"NYP plates," he pointed out, the prefix "NYP" in New York State license plates meaning the working press. "You aren't the only one around here with clout, baby."

"Come on, Terry," I said. "Lay off."

Then he laughed, and even through the phone I could feel him relaxing. "Sorry," he said. "I got up on the wrong side of the bed this morning. When *you* get up, try the right."

"Thanks for the tip."

"See you later."

"See you."

I gave the phone back to Anita, who hung it up and said, "What was that all about?"

"Terry wants to take me out to the Island to talk to somebody about pharmaceutical companies."

Surprised, she said, "Really? Why now all of a sudden?"

In order to get out of bed on the right side I would have to climb over Anita, which would be pleasant for me, but confusing for her. Staying where I was, I said, "I guess it's a result of last night's conversation."

Anita nodded. "Tell him he's on a list of murder suspects and he decides to be helpful."

"A very mature reaction."

"Better than a poke in the mouth," she agreed, "the reaction I myself am still considering. You want coffee?"

"In a little while," I said.

36

In some ways, the conversation with Morton Adler was very satisfactory. To begin with, he took the subject much less personally than anyone else I'd talked to so far. I laid out the situation simply and unemotionally, as I would if it were any normal legal problem I was bringing him for solution, and he listened, nodding, making no comment till the end, when all he said was, "We will never know the inmost heart of any other human being, will we?"

"No, we never will."

He considered the case. "Going about the problem the way you are is probably the best way to gather information and narrow the list of suspects," he decided, "but then what?"

"What do you mean?"

"When you have your package assembled—assuming that's possible, which it may not be—but when you do have it assembled, what will you do with it?"

"I'll cross that bridge when I come to it."

"Please, Sam," he said. "Phone me before you cross the bridge." Then he expressed amusement in his usual manner, by looking down, smiling shyly, and nodding several times. "Unless I turn out to be the murderer, of course."

That *was* a ridiculous idea, dammit. A short and stocky man in his mid-fifties, Morton Adler looks more like an unworldly college professor—maybe of anthropology—than the tough and brilliant lawyer he actually is. His neat round head is crosshatched by thin but still-black hair, he reacts to everything with the same careful slowness, and he knows so much I sometimes think he swallowed the encyclopedia whole. This man doing the bidding of Frank Althorn, or some other mob thug? No way.

I said, "Last night, Gretchen Young told me she was talking with you during the time when Doug was being killed."

"Oh, did she? Very nice of her." He nodded again, looking at the jumble of *things* on his desk—Morton is not a neat man—and then slowly said, "That would be with the other two women, as well. One in television, and one in social work."

Which is what Gretchen had said. "Ann Goodman and Helen Mayhew."

"Yes, that's right. And the striking woman in fashion."

"Vera Slote."

"We were talking about travel in Europe."

"That's right."

He cocked his head, giving me a bright-eyed look. "I agree with Gretchen, do I? Sam, never believe two witnesses. Always triangulate. Two people can collude, but a scheme involving three always has loose threads." Picking up the phone on his desk, he said, "Go over to the table there, be ready to pick up when I tell you."

The second phone in the room was on a refectory table

under the windows, among messy piles of contracts, wills, correspondence, forms, newspapers, books, and general detritus. I went over there, glanced out at the view from above of Grand Central Station hunched among all the new tall buildings, then turned back to watch Morton turn through his Rolodex, pause, and dial a number. "Miss Goodman, please," he said, and nodded at me to pick up.

Which I did, in time to hear a nasal male voice say, "Miss Goodman's office."

"Morton Adler for Miss Goodman."

Click. Pause. Ann Goodman's voice: "Morton Adler? Sam Holt's friend?"

"That's right. We met at that tragic party at Sam's."

"Do you know I had bad dreams for a week? Drowning in waterfalls. What can I do for you?"

"Just before you went away and made that, well, that discovery, we'd been talking about visits to Europe."

"That's right, I remember that."

"You and your friend, uh . . . Is it Helen?"

"Helen Mayhew, yes. And Gretchen Young was with us, Terry Young's wife."

Morton smiled across the room at me, then smiled shyly at the floor, as he said, "Was she? I'd forgotten that. But there was a place you were talking about that night—"

"Yes?"

"On the French Riviera, but in a few miles from the Med. A restaurant and hotel you said was charming. I've been trying to remember the name."

"Oh, you must mean the Ponte Romano!"

"I knew it had a bridge in it," Morton said, with a sly look in my direction.

"Yes, they actually still do have an ancient Roman bridge right there on the property, over the little stream, just beside the swimming pool. It's in a place called Plan De La Tour, a tiny, tiny town away from *everywhere*. When are you planning to go?''

"Oh, not me. A friend of mine.''

"I hope it's a good friend. I don't want to tell just anybody about that place.''

"I'll swear him to absolute secrecy.''

I looked out the window at the clear pale sky and the gray buildings and the green metal roofs down below. Morton, Gretchen, Ann, and Helen were now all off the list. To narrow it that surely and that much all at once was a real step forward.

On the other hand, there were still six names on the list and they composed a group that did not at all please me: Anita, Terry, Maria, Vera Slote, and the Hendersons, Nora and Jerry. Would tonight's dinner with the Hendersons narrow it even more—and more unhappily—or end the need for lists at all?

Morton had finished his conversation. We both hung up, and Morton got to his feet. Coming around the desk, a short, compact, completely self-assured man, he said, "If it were me, I'd try for at least one more independent verification.''

"Morton,'' I said, "are you trying to help, or are you putting me on?''

"Both.'' He smiled at the floor, shaking his head, and said, "Sam, I do agree with what you're doing so far, since you can't get the problem out of your mind, though, to be honest, I wouldn't have recommended this course of action if you'd asked my advice. But before you come to any final conclusions, or *act*, take any action at *all*, beyond questions and interviews, please, please get in touch with me.''

I had to grin at him. "A stitch in time, eh?''

He patted my arm. "Less work for mother,'' he said.

37

Armed with his NYP plates, Terry was parked directly in front of the entrance, in one of the most stringent "No Stopping" zones in the city, at Lexington Avenue and 44th, next to the eastern entry to Grand Central Station. Cabs angled around him, pedestrians passed to both sides like a stream bubbling by a boulder, and buses kept threatening his driver's side mirror, but Terry sat, calm and uncaring, reading this morning's late edition of his own paper.

I'm in the habit of crossing the sidewalk at a fast pace, to discourage celebrity grabbers, so I did that now, striding through the messengers, tourists, salesmen, models, lawyers, three-card-monte players, job seekers, suburban shoppers, and truants that make up this neighborhood's normal population at ten-thirty of a weekday morning, being ignored, by the way, by them all. Without pausing, I pulled open the passenger door.

Terry looked at me mildly over his paper as I slid briskly onto the seat, folding my legs into the small space under the

glove compartment as I slammed the door. "Pants on fire?"
he asked me.

"No," I said. "How about yours?"

He grinned. "Not anymore."

"Glad to hear it. Anything good in the paper?"

"Nah." He dumped it in my lap and started the engine,
and we made our way away from there.

Hands on the folded paper in my lap, I said, "Where are
we going?"

"To see Congressman Toomey," he said, as though that
explained everything.

"Oh, sure," I said. "Come on, Terry, don't be a wise
guy."

"Let me deal with this goddamn traffic a minute, okay?
Let me get through the tunnel, then we'll talk."

So I left him alone to shoulder his way through the traffic
to the Midtown Tunnel, while I leafed through his paper and
found he had a byline story about arson-for-hire in Brooklyn.
This was meat and potatoes stuff that Terry tosses off with no
trouble at all, combining hints of the tough guy with touches
of literary background. I read it without a lot of interest, but
admiring again his mastery of that particularly odd style, and
when I finished, we were in the tunnel. "I suppose now
you'll want to wait till we pay the toll," I said.

"Yes. Do you have any change?"

Between us, we had just enough coins to make it possible
to go through the exact-change lane. Then as we took the
curving sweep up to the elevated road of the Long Island
Expressway, moderately full but fast-moving at this hour,
Terry—watching traffic while he spoke—said, "Don Toomey
is a liberal Republican congressman out on the Island. You
have to be a Republican out there, but you don't have to be a
liberal, so he's refreshing in some ways. He's been elected
five times, so he's got a little seniority by now and can have

some say in the subjects he'll take an interest in. One of the subjects he takes a great deal of interest in is the export of American pharmaceuticals."

"Ah-hah," I said.

"I met him a few years ago," Terry told me, "doing a Sunday piece on congressmen in the sticks outside the five boroughs. We got along, we kept in touch."

"Even though you're not much use to each other."

He gave me a surprised, then amused, look. "That's right. My readers can't vote for him, and his clout doesn't extend to my regular beat."

"So you actually like each other."

"It happens," Terry said. "Anyway, I gave him a transcript of your testimony at the inquest, all about everything your pal Doug told you on the famous walk on the beach, and he became very, very interested in the idea of talking to you."

"When?"

Again he glanced away from traffic to give me a look of brief surprise. "Now," he said. "That's where we're going."

"No. I mean, when did you give him the transcript?"

"Last month. Oh, you want to know why he's so hot all of a sudden."

"Yes."

"I phoned him this morning," Terry told me, keeping an eye on the traffic. "Told him you were playing Packard, explained the situation, told him about you eating my food last night while accusing my wife and me of murdering old friends of yours in your house. He said he wanted to meet anybody who had that much chutzpah. I said I'd arrange it." He looked away from the surrounding trucks and cars one more time to give me a jaundiced look, saying, "I don't see what there is to laugh about, frankly."

38

The two parts of Long Island I know are Mineola, barely beyond the New York City line, and the Hamptons, way out on the South Shore, where friends of mine have summer places. Other than that, I know mostly that the Island *is* long: one hundred thirty miles from the East River across Queens and out across Nassau and Suffolk counties to Montauk Point. The North Shore, separated from Connecticut by the sailboat-filled civilized expanse of Long Island Sound, is richer and more socially prominent, the middle is bedroom communities for commuters from New York, and the South Shore is a broad mix, from boatyards and clam diggers to lush estates.

It was to the South Shore we went, forty-five minutes out from the city. "The congressman has a boat," Terry explained on the way out. "It's a great place for a private conversation."

It turned out to be a fine place, if a boat can be a place, whether for conversation or anything else. We left the high-

way at last and drove down to and through a sleepy South
Shore town, with glimpses of the water of the Great South
Bay glinting ahead of us in the June sunlight. Nearly to the
shore, we turned in at a muddy driveway under an arched
sign that read "Morrison's Boatyard." Making our way among
cars and pickups and campers parked any which way on the
mud and grass, Terry steered us around an old clapboard
house that had been converted to shops and offices, then
came to a stop next to a tall corrugated-iron structure painted
a faded blue. A broad channel in from the bay was visible
ahead, dotted with small boats of various kinds. "Try to
walk *above* the mud," Terry advised, as we got out.

Not easy to do. An L-shaped wooden pier, old and gray,
extended out into the channel, then made a right turn toward
the bay. Pausing to kick mud off my shoes onto the boards of
the pier, I followed Terry out almost to the end of the L,
where a gleaming two-story inboard powerboat was tied up.
It was mostly white, with touches of chrome and rich blue,
all spotlessly clean and shining. Up on the flying bridge, a
man in yellow polo shirt and tan slacks was polishing something with a rag. When Terry yelled, "Ho, the Jolly Roger!
Permission to come aboard!" the man looked around at us,
grinned, and waved a welcome with the rag.

Jolly Roger? I looked at the stern as we boarded, and the
name was really *Mary, Mary.* Quite contrary? I noticed
the congressman was not a tax evader, was not registered in
Wilmington, Delaware, but in Sayville, New York.

He came down the ladder from the bridge as we boarded,
and turned a smiling quizzical face toward me, waiting for
Terry's introduction. A tanned, square-jawed, well-built man
of about forty, with wavy black hair and an easily confident
smile full of gleaming teeth, he was saved from prettiness by
a lumpily comical nose and very thick black eyebrows, making him ninety percent Irish charmer and ten percent Irish

clown; just about the right percentage for a politician, I thought, as Terry said, "Congressman, this is the upstart actor I told you about. Sam Holt, Don Toomey."

We shook hands, his grip firm but not challenging, and he grinned at me as he said, "I don't get to look *up* at many people. Do you absolutely have to be that tall?"

"I tend to shrink toward evening," I assured him. He was about six three, so I probably was an unusual experience for him, and it was interesting that it troubled him enough to make a joke about it at the very beginning.

"I look forward to evening," he told me, and turned away to call, "Claire!"

"Oh, is she here?" Terry asked. He sounded pleased.

"She'll run the boat," Toomey told him, "while we all talk man talk."

Meanwhile, out from the companionway was stepping a tall slender woman with ash-blond hair pulled back and held with a red rubber band. She wore scuffed sneakers, white shorts, and a pale blue polo shirt. I guessed her at mid-thirties, attractive in a cool-looking way, with a long and rangy body. "My wife," Toomey announced, smiling with pleasure at the idea. "Claire, this is Sam Holt."

"Of course it is," she said, and stuck out a slim hand to be shaken. "You're even more awe-inspiring in person," she told me.

Aware of Toomey watching, prepared to be amused at my discomfiture in the face of his wife's forthrightness, I merely returned her smile, shook her hand, bowed slightly, and said, "I do have a reputation to uphold."

"Foisted on you by people like Terry, I'm sure," she said, smiling, releasing my hand.

"Hey!" Terry said. "How did *I* get into this?"

"She's a very wise lady," I told him.

"Wise enough to quit when I'm ahead," Claire Toomey

said, and turned to her husband, saying, "You want me to
take the tiller?"

"Yes, please."

I helped in taking off the lines holding us to the dock,
while Claire Toomey went up to the bridge and started the
motor, causing a feline growl to start below the rear of the
boat, accompanied by bubbles, as though some sea monster,
half whale and half lion, were imprisoned down there.

The *Mary, Mary* eased out into the channel. Claire Toomey
up top perched on a wooden stool as she drove, the rest of us
settling into blue canvas chairs in the cockpit at the rear.
Sailboats and other motorboats were all around us, some
moored, some in motion, their owners taking advantage of
this warm spring day. On the way out the channel Toomey
led the conversation, telling us he'd been brought up farther
out this same shoreline, in Bellport, and had been in love
with small boats on this bay all his life. "You're from
somewhere on the Island, aren't you, Sam?" he then asked,
which led into a casual but fairly thorough exchange of our
backgrounds, with Terry adding an occasional comment or
question of his own.

When we left the channel and moved out into the slightly
choppy waters of the bay, Fire Island was a low dark line
across the way, part of the southern edge of this body of
water. Out of sight, just a bit to the west of here, was Jones
Beach, where Doug and I had talked the night I'd met him.
Claire Toomey set our course in that direction, toward Robert
Moses Causeway, visible a few miles ahead, and her husband
got down to business. "I understand from Terry," he said,
"that your interest in this matter is personal."

"That's right."

"A friend was killed. Another friend, apparently, has sold
you out in some way."

"Apparently," I agreed.

"Good," Toomey said, with a down-patting gesture, as though stowing one wrapped-up package away to make room for the next problem. "Let me tell you, then, what *my* interest is."

"Sure."

"My interest is impersonal," he told me. "In fact, it's global." But he smiled and shook his head as he said it, as though to defuse any idea that he wanted to be pretentious. "And," he went on, "as far as I'm concerned, my interest is a nice combination of humanitarianism and sensible political reality. My thrust here is those areas we commonly call the Third World."

"Yes?"

"Yes. We're in a situation, Sam, where . . . It's all right to call you Sam?"

"Of course," I said.

"And I'm Don. Anyway, the paradox of our time is that suddenly strength is weakness, which necessarily makes weakness strength. What I'm saying is . . ." he said, leaning closer to me, marking off items on his fingers, unconsciously turning our conversation into a debate, "what I'm saying is, we and the Russians are the big guys on the block, the bullies, the strongest players in the game by far, but the problem now is that our strength can't be used. Whoever starts a nuclear war loses in the first instant of hostilities—in fact, we all lose—and most of us, thank God, realize that."

"We're a long way from pharmaceuticals," I pointed out, grinning to take the sting out of it.

"Bear with me," he said, and went on, obviously used to people bearing with him. "Once you take the source of our great strength out of play," he said, "all of a sudden we're on a par footing with a lot of the little guys. We still have technology, industry, and a trained population, but they're busily getting those things, too."

"With our help," Terry put in.

"Of course," Don Toomey answered. "The concept is that we would rather share the world with educated friendlies than hostile barbarians. If everybody's doing reasonably well, there won't be enough envy in the world to cause a whole lot of trouble. But a key element in the equation," he said, turning back to me, "is educated *friendlies*. What if, on the one hand, we train them and equip them and arm them, while, on the other hand, we insult and abuse and maim them?"

"Not smart," I said.

"No. But it's what we're doing. And this brings us to your pharmaceuticals, Sam, because what's happening, I'm afraid, is that we are shitting on the Third World. Almost literally, we are dumping our shit on those people."

"Bad drugs, you mean?"

"Pesticides we've banned domestically, for example," he said, "but can still make a profit selling in Africa and South America. Questionable medicines that can't pass the FDA tests, or decent medicines mislabeled for use in ways where they don't do anybody any good. Products we won't put in *our* bodies or our air or our water or our soil, and we're shipping them overseas. And experimental drugs, experimental medicines, too; try them on pregnant women in Uruguay and Uganda, and if nothing goes too terribly wrong, *then* you go through the expense of passing U.S. government tests."

Though Toomey was clearly impassioned about all this, there was a practiced ring to what he was saying, a prepared-speech effect; the alliteration of the country names, for instance. This was part of a speech he sometimes delivered, or an op-ed article in the *Times*, or a fund-raising letter to his big-ticket supporters. Which didn't, of course, take away from his sincerity. However, there was another problem I thought I saw, and so I said, "Most of this is legal, isn't it?"

"Most of it is legal in the consumer nations," he said, "though not all of it. Some of it is legal in the producer nations, both in Europe and here, but nowhere *near* all of it. Much more should be illegal, and we're working on it. *I'm* working on it, for whatever good that might do. I'm a cosponsor of three pieces of legislation in this area, and do you know what bothers me, Sam?"

"No, I don't," I said, not telling him that what bothers *me* is the rhetorical question.

"How my support slides away," he said, and spread his arms out to the sides, wiggling his fingers as though shaking water off them. "On Monday we'll have the votes, and by Wednesday they'll be gone. I want to start hearings on this subject, and I'm being blocked in strange ways and from strange directions. The last congressional study in this area was thirty years ago, chaired by Senator Estes Kefauver. It brought out some of the problems, some of the abuses, but by no means all of them. I want to pick it up from there, and I'm running into blank walls, and when Terry showed me your statement to the inquest, I began to see the light. If the companies I'm concerned about are linked in an underhanded way to elements in national government, and at the same time they're tied in with organized crime, then the wall of silence and indifference I've been running into starts to make some sense."

"If," I said.

"Well, here's the other part of it," he said. "Every over-the-counter drug sold in this country—not Third World now, *this* country—has federal agency approval. The applications and the testing are expensive. Drugs have failed to get on the market not because there was anything provably wrong with them but simply because the approval process was too time-consuming and expensive for the potential profits from selling the product. Now, what if two companies are about to launch essentially similar products? What if one of those companies sails through the testing and approval process, while the other company has to keep going back to redo things, provide more test results, consider more variables? The first company could be on the market five *years* before the second.''

"So,'' I said, "a company with an undercover link somewhere high in government—''

"Could destroy its competition,'' Toomey said, "much more directly and completely than in any other business I can think of. Profits on legal drugs and medicines are *huge;* if they're funneled increasingly into one area of the market, and if that market is controlled by organized crime, it's an extremely dangerous situation, and we ought to know about it.''

"The idea of links between organized crime and this person or that person in the federal government has been suggested before,'' I said.

He nodded. "But it's this third link in the chain that makes it so scary. Bringing in the pharmaceuticals. You can choose whether or not to gamble, whether or not to visit a whore. When you're sick, you *need* the medicine. And you need that government watchdog to keep everything safe. Your friend believed that three-way link exists, and he believed he could prove it.''

"At least one of the people doing some work for him was sure he never would,'' I said. "I do believe Doug saw something, and then he *knew,* or at least he thought he knew, but he was nowhere near proving it.''

"Near enough to be killed,'' Toomey said.

"Doug himself said that would be a preemptive strike, putting him away before he became dangerous.''

"Terry tells me you've done some follow-up on that,'' Toomey said. He made no patronizing reference to Packard, for which I was grateful. "I'm wondering," he said, "if you'll share with me whatever you've learned."

"Which isn't much," I said. "And, in any case, I've mostly concentrated on the murder itself, not on the conspiracy or whatever it is that Doug was after."

"Whatever you've done," he said. "I'd appreciate anything you want to tell me."

I shrugged. "Well, it won't take long," I said, and started in with what had happened in San Francisco. I'd related Joe Kearny's opinion that the whole thing was a fool's errand, and was in the middle of describing the blank wall I'd bumped into in connection with Okushiri International Forwarding, when Claire Toomey came down from the bridge to announce we were "here." I looked around as Don Toomey dropped the plow anchor, and "here" turned out to be nowhere in particular; out in the middle of the bay, beyond the Robert Moses Causeway, with Fire Island Inlet on our left and Long Island on our right. There were no other boats moored nearby, which was pleasant, though back by the bridge a bunch of small craft was gathered together in an area that was presumably good fishing.

"Here" was also where we had lunch, both Toomeys bringing out salads and rolls and iced tea from within, the four of us sitting companionably in the cockpit. I continued my story, both Don and Claire interrupting with a question from time to time, Terry occasionally adding a footnote to my narrative, and when lunch and I were both finished, Don Toomey said, "Well, we're both of us pretty much in the dark, it looks like."

"I see plenty of smoke," I said, "so I suppose there must be a fire, but darned if I can find it."

"I need to find that fire, Sam," he said, with a kind of stagy intensity. "If I can get some movement in the House, on any one of my bills or even better on the hearings, a whole lot of misery and bitterness in this world can be avoided. I'm not exactly a freshman down there, but there are nearly five hundred of us in the club and there are times when one man absolutely can*not* make a difference. If I can define the enemy, get a handle on him and a look at him, I'll be better able to keep my own troops in line, and not lose them to business-as-usual."

I shook my head, saying, "I don't know what I can do to help."

"You're positive there's no point following Doug Walford's trail anymore, is that right?"

"No, there's no point," I said. "I trust Kearny's opinion on that."

"So what's left," Toomey said, "is the murder. That's our best hope, Sam."

"I guess it is," I agreed.

He leaned toward me, nodding, watching me, willing me to succeed. "When you've got the murderer," he said, "you'll have whoever hired him or ordered him. And maybe *that's* the piece of thread that'll help us unravel the whole fabric."

"Wouldn't that be nice," I said.

39

The subject matter was grim, but the day itself was pleasant enough, and at least a physical respite. In late afternoon, the sun behind us, we rode back to the Toomeys' mooring, and Terry and I made our departure. Driving back toward the city against the growing buildup of traffic coming out, we discussed the congressman and his wife, agreeing they were nice people, agreeing that Don Toomey was overly theatrical but nevertheless sincere, and speculating on just which companies or individuals might be involved in the conspiracy Doug thought he'd found. We didn't talk directly about Doug's murder or about the list of remaining suspects, because of course Terry was still—absurdly, ridiculously, but necessarily—on it. Along with Anita and Maria Kaiser and Vera Slote and the Hendersons.

After Terry dropped me at my place, and while I was changing for dinner, I found myself wishing the murderer would turn out to be Vera Slote after all, despite her successful career as a clothing designer, simply because I knew her the least of the remaining group. But that wouldn't help either, would it? If Vera were guilty, then Bill Ackerson, who'd brought her, was also guilty. A fashion designer and a successful New York doctor—sure.

Tonight we had a successful director and a moderately successful actress, Jerry and Nora Henderson, she using the professional name Nora Battle. She was a character woman, the round-faced pretty blonde who's always confused, always prattling, hands waving in the air, hopeless with all known machinery, breasts constantly about to fall out of her clothing. The "character" that character actors hone and polish for themselves is usually some altered or simplified version of their real persona, and so it was with Nora Henderson, who was a shrewd but still physically awkward version of Nora Battle. The constant excessive hand gestures, threatening every lamp and drink and whatnot in sight, carried over into real life, and so did the wide-eyed trustful gaze. The grating voice and the armory of lower-class accents and the general ditziness all disappeared, however, as did the impression that luscious globes were about to burst from the blouse; at home, Nora spoke normal middle-class American speech, had a brain in her head, and dressed like a grown-up.

She it was who met Anita and me at the door and ushered us into their new apartment. "We're a mess," she said. "We're still a mess. We're *always* a mess. Well, you know us. *And* we just moved in. Well, three months ago." And her hands waved throughout, fingers flickering like butterfly impersonations.

She was right about the apartment being a mess. Earlier this year, when Jerry finally decided he could make more money (and no less respect or esteem) directing commercials in New York than TV episodes in Los Angeles, they'd moved back East, taking this ninth-floor apartment in a fairly new building on East 19th Street. Inside, the large L-shaped living-dining room was severely underfurnished. The mover's cartons—*Mayflower*, they all said—stacked on their sides along one interior wall, had become bookcases and knick-knack shelves. The parquet-veneer floor was bare, and half a dozen mismatched chairs—including a red metal folding chair—stood around on it with an equally varied assortment of lamps and side tables. Over by the broad south-facing windows—the view was mostly of the lit-up Con Edison building tower down on 14th Street—it was hard to tell exactly what sort of table was under the very good old linen cloth, except that it had heavy wooden X-style legs, like lawn furniture. A blown-up poster-style still frame from that portion of a PACKARD intro with *Directed by Jerry Henderson* superimposed was the only wall decoration.

Nora guided our choice of seats, took our drink orders, and went away to the kitchen as Jerry came out, in white chef's cap and an apron covered with comical references to barbecues—left over from their California life, I suppose—to welcome us, grinning, kissing his fingertips, saying, "For the food you are about to eat, you will die, die, die." Jerry does all the cooking in the Henderson household, with gusto and high good humor and generally good results. (The first thing Nora does, every time she enters a kitchen for any reason other than to make a drink, is cut her thumb.)

Anita said, "What nation tonight, Jerry?" because Jerry's specialty is menus from all over the world.

"Brazil," he said. "Portuguese and Indian influences, but its *own* thing. You're going to love it and love it and love it." A tall shambling man with lots of curly red hair and an almost manic gleam of pleasure in his eyes, Jerry overstated as naturally as breathing.

We assured him we were looking forward to a Brazilian dinner, and asked him what he was up to at the moment, and he told a very funny story about a bubble-making machine

running amok on a residential street in New Hyde Park out
on Long Island during the filming of a cleanser commercial.
By then, Nora was back with our drinks—and her own rum
and water—permitting Jerry to return to the kitchen.

Jerry had not apologized for the appearance of the apartment or commented on it in any way, and that was typical of
the man. As a director, both of television shows and commercials, he was known as a lyrical artist with the camera
and a strong and supportive and useful worker with actors,
but his great flaw was that he never cared about, never even
seemed to notice, what the surrounding environment *looked
like*. In a typical Jerry Henderson scene, well-rehearsed and
comfortable actors would be shown to best advantage, and
nuances of story-line demonstrated cleanly and without fuss,
against a background completely irrelevant to, or possibly
even contradictory of, what was happening up front.

In episodic TV, where most of the sets are already a part
of the ongoing series—Packard's office, for instance, or the
living room in any sitcom—that gap in his talent and vision
didn't matter so much (though his exteriors, where a set
designer wouldn't be around to save him, were usually excru-
ciatingly flat and dull). In commercials, on the other hand,
where the environment matters a *lot*, there were always any
number of agency and product people around to make sure
the appearance of the background supported the subliminal
message. So in neither case was he badly hampered by this
complete indifference to the look of the world around him. (It
did explain, however, why he could never hope to make a
career with TV movies-of-the-week or feature films.)

Jerry's indifference to appearances, when combined with
Nora's physical ineptitude and somewhat scatterbrained treatment of the world beyond her own career, did mean that their
homes tended to be a little odd. The red metal folding chair
in this place, and the trestle table under linen, and the

packer's cardboard cartons used as bookcases, were all par for the course; this was by no means the strangest home setting in which I'd ever visited the Hendersons.

Nora and Anita and I made unimportant shoptalk until Jerry announced dinner, at which point we each carried our chair over to the table, where Nora placed us, boy-girl-boy-girl. (No one had chosen the red metal folding chair, which was left in the other part of the L to carry on conversation with the blue Amish rocker with the hex sign on its back.)

While Jerry brought out a large covered tureen smelling pleasantly of beans and spices, Nora opened a Chilean jug wine called Concha y Toro, which claimed to be a blending of cabernet sauvignon and merlot, and which turned out to be heavy but good. Jerry's second trip to the kitchen produced a platter artfully arranged with various kinds of stewed meat—Canadian bacon, beef, pork, and two kinds of sausage—all displayed around a central flourish of smoked tongue. The tureen, when Nora started serving us, contained a heavy broth filled with black beans and onions. Jerry, piling meats on and around the beans on our plates, said, "This is the national dish of Brazil. It's called," and then he said, "Fay," and then he cleared his throat, and then he said, "oh," and then he said, "dah," and then he said, "I have no idea if I'm pronouncing it right." So he spelled it for us; "F-e-i-j-o-a-d-a."

Whatever it was called, and wherever it was from, it was delicious. Back when I was on PACKARD there was an older guy, a production assistant, who used to mourn the good old days, when he'd worked on *I Spy* and, even before that, *Foreign Intrigue*, both series that had spent most of their time on location. "Never mind the sights," he used to say, "all that tourist crap. The *food*—that's what I miss. And look at me now, trapped in the land of sand dabs and Cobb salad." I told the Hendersons about him now, and said, "I think I begin to understand what he was talking about."

Jerry beamed with pleasure under all that red hair, while Nora said, "A fine hand with a compliment."

"It's sincere."

Jerry said, "This isn't really authentic, I have to admit. I left out the pig's foot."

"It's close enough," Anita assured him.

"The wine is inauthentic, too," Nora told us, gesturing this way and that, eyes and pendant earrings sparkling. "We should be drinking a *cachaça*, Brazilian rum. Jerry wanted to, but I said we should adapt to local customs. Wine with dinner, rum with suntans."

"All the authentic stuff comes from Casa Moneo down on Fourteenth Street," Jerry told us. "Terrific Latin American supermarket."

The food was first-rate, but pretty heavy going for June, and I was glad when dessert turned out to be a mango sherbet, plus strong coffee. And, if we wanted it, cocaine. "A little nose candy to top off the meal?" Jerry asked, looking around brightly at us.

"Is it authentic?" I asked him.

"Well, it's from *somewhere* south of the border," he said. "Very clean nice stuff. Impeccable source, medically approved. Isn't that right, Nora?"

Nora paused in clearing the table to agree. I said, "Not tonight, thanks, Jerry," and Anita also refused.

Why is it that the offerer of cocaine never feels awkward, but the refuser always does? It's allied, I guess, to not accepting a dare in grade school. On the other hand, part of growing up is learning which dares *not* to accept, and drugs are well up on the list of things to outgrow. Several of the people connected with PACKARD were high most of the time; the agent for some of our actors doubled as a dealer, and there was always a general sense of swimming in a secret giggly sea of drug culture. I finally came to the conclusion that cocaine was the only way heterosexuals had of having a hip private club, and that it was okay not to want to join.

The Hendersons weren't pushers, merely thoughtful hosts. They accepted our refusal of cocaine as readily as if we'd said no to the coffee or sherbet. Their separate brief retirements to the bedroom at the end of dinner were discreet, and neither seemed particularly changed afterward. We carried our chairs back to the living-room area, and again tonight it was Anita who raised the subject of the party and Doug Walford's death. When she did, Jerry sat up straighter and said, "I never figured that out. There was *something* going on there, but it was like the middle of my script was gone. What was it, Sam? Did he OD?"

"No," I said, "he was—"

Nora said, "Andy Margran OD'd, you know," referring to an actor with whom I'd worked a few times in the old days.

"Did he? I knew he'd died, but I didn't know what of."

"Bill Ackerson told us," Jerry said. The Hendersons were also patients of Bill's, through my recommendation.

"He didn't mention it to me," I said.

Nora giggled, and Jerry said, "The family went crazy. They covered up like mad, kept it all a deep dark secret, and now everybody thinks Andy died of AIDS."

"What's a mother to do?" Nora asked, waving her arms and grinning at us all.

"They can't run around and *tell* everybody," Jerry pointed out, and did a high-pitched frantic imitation: " 'My son wasn't a faggot, he was a *junkie!*' Oh, the truth is best, it really is."

"Because it won't out, you know," Nora told us, suddenly solemn. "That's the bitch of it. Truth will not out. In fact, truth is very *hard* to come by."

"I'll go along with that," I said. "Doug Walford, for instance, was murdered."

They stared at me, with almost identical comic open-mouthed expressions. Jerry, in hushed tones, said, "By whom?"

"Somebody at the party."

"Which one?" Nora asked.

"I don't know yet. That's the hard truth I'm working on."

Anita said, "What it comes down to is trying to figure out where everybody was just before the murder. For instance, Nora, you and I were together for a while."

Nora blinked at her. "Were we? Well, we must have been. I mean, I talked with everybody; I feel the whole point of a party is to talk to *everybody*. Except your husband, of course."

"Har-har," Jerry said, and winked at me.

"Well, you did talk to your husband," Anita told her. "You and I talked for a while, and then Jerry came over and you told him it was time to go home."

"She always says that," Jerry said, "and she's always wrong."

"Not always, Jerry," Nora said. "I've seen you be wonderful at a party, and then all of a sudden you're not Mr. Wonderful anymore." To us, still smiling and sparkly, she said, "No complaints. I've been known to leave wonderfulness behind myself, once or twice. Just little bits." She wiggled her fingers.

Jerry said, "Oh, I remember, you thought I was coming on to Brett Burgess's wife."

"Maria Kaiser," I said. "They're not married."

"If I thought you were," Nora told him, "you were."

"I plead *non compos mentis*," Jerry told her. "As usual." Grinning at Anita, he said, "That's what she was saying, wasn't it? Big eyes for the photographer lady."

"That was probably after I left you both to go get another drink."

I said, "So I guess you two were still together when the word came down about Doug."

"Yes," Nora said, absolutely positive. "I remember I said, 'See? I *knew* it was time to go.' "

"So we alibi each other, honeybunch," Jerry told her, and grinned at me. "Isn't that right?"

Nora said, "Wives don't alibi or testify or whatever it is."

"Then husbands won't either," Jerry told her.

Anita said, "The awful thing is, it has to be one of us."

Jerry stared owlishly at her. "One of us four?"

"Not quite," Anita said, and I could see her trying not to laugh. "But somebody at the party."

"A *friend?*" Jerry's stare turned to me. "A friend of *yours?*"

"Looks that way."

"That's awful," Nora said.

"Yes, it is."

Jerry said, "You mean, somebody there had a grudge against this fellow, this, . . ."

"Doug Walford. It wasn't a grudge; it was a contract killing."

"Mobsters?" Jerry goggled. "*You* don't know any mobsters!"

"Apparently," I said, "I know somebody the mobsters could use."

"Oh." Jerry sat back, thinking about that. "Hmmmm," he said.

"Pressures," Nora commented, slowly, thoughtfully. Her hands rested in her lap. "They can be awful, you know? Pressure to do this, do that. You don't always get to do what you want."

"That's true," I said.

"But you get what you need," she said.

Jerry got up and switched to the blue fake Amish rocker and sat down. We all attended to him. Rocking back and forth, frowning at me, he said, "I'm thinking about this like a script, Sam, you know? Like it's a PACKARD. You know the first thing I'd do?"

"What?"

"I'd go over the script, I'd get it rewritten if I had to, I'd make sure I had that pressure right in there. Up front. That pressure, that sense of doom. The *killer* is the doomed one, driven to do things he *hates*."

"Sympathy for the murderer," I suggested.

"Symphony for the devil," Nora murmured.

Jerry said, "Well, sure, isn't that the way to play it?" He grinned at me, raised a hand, made a kind of doorknob-turning gesture. "Twist the old story," he said. "Here's the murderer, between a rock and a hard place, can't get out of trouble. Here's the relentless Packard, gonna track him down. Wait!" He sat up, the rocker creaking. "How about this? The murderer didn't sign on to commit murder! Just to—I don't know—take pictures? Pass along a warning? Maybe break kneecaps, something like that, leave it to the writer for the details. The point is, it's the step-step-step down to doom. Before the murderer knows it, he's in so deep he can't get back out. You've got a guy, he's an ordinary guy, he's almost, you know, admirable—"

"Like you and me," I suggested.

"Right. If the mob goes to this guy and says, 'Here's some poison; off that fella at the party,' he's gonna say, 'That's not on my resumé. I don't do windows, I don't do murder.' So they tell him, do this other thing, something less, see?"

"I see," I said.

"Something he *can* do," Jerry went on. "And he does it. Then the next step, and the next."

"Drawn in," I said.

"That's a pretty story," Jerry said, smiling, admiring it. "Lots of tension, viewer identification."

"With the murderer."

"Sure!" Jerry grinned around at us, and saw Nora gazing at him with a very troubled look. His grin faltered and he looked at Anita, and then at me. "Well, it's just a *story*," he said.

40

Bill Ackerson and Anita and I were scheduled to have lunch the next day at Vitto Impero, one of those rare instances when Anita would become a customer in her own joint. I was a few minutes late because I got two phone calls just as I was leaving the house, both of them of interest.

The first was Vera Slote, back from Paris. In fact, just barely back from Paris. "I haven't been to the office yet," she said, "but I phoned and they said you'd been by."

"If we could spend ten or fifteen minutes together, I'd appreciate it," I suggested. "I'm sorry, it's hard to explain on the phone."

"I *must* go to the office this afternoon," she told me, "but we might have drinks after."

"Sorry, no, I'm going out of town. Just overnight." Because tonight was when Sandy Sheriff was to introduce me to Frank Althorn.

"What about tomorrow, then?"

"Fine. Should I bring Bill?"

"Oh, well, Bill," she said. "That isn't . . . Well, that wouldn't be necessary."

I grinned; Bill had a never-ending supply of attractive women to escort here and there, but none of the relationships lasted very long. "Without Bill, then," I said.

"I'll be in the office all day tomorrow. Could you pick me up there?"

"Of course."

"Five-thirty?"

"Fine."

"I'm afraid," she said, "I already have dinner plans."

"I'm sure you're busy," I told her, "just back in town, and all that. I'm glad you can spare time for a drink."

"Well, I'm intrigued, naturally. And . . . Would it be terrible to say it? I did enjoy the party at your house, until the tragedy at the finish."

"Yes."

"And the house itself. Very stylish, very good. We might have a minute or two to talk about that as well."

"We might," I agreed, and reconfirmed that I'd meet her at her office tomorrow at five-thirty, and we hung up. And I was almost to the front door when the phone rang again. I very nearly went on, leaving it to the answering machine to deal with whoever it was, but then I thought it might be Vera Slote calling back to change our appointment, so I gave up and answered and it was Bly, calling from home, before leaving for the studio. "Hello," I said. "How goes *Akers' Acres*?"

"Achingly. How goes the investigation?"

"Muddlingly."

"You were on the phone when I called before."

"Just a few minutes ago? That was one of my suspects, Vera Slote."

"The fashion designer? Should I be jealous?"

"I don't think so," I said. "Not yet, anyway. I'm having drinks with her tomorrow, so maybe after that."

"Here's looking at *you*, kid."

"I'll feel your eyes on me every second."

"Vera Slote *is* a very good-looking woman, in an exotic way," Bly said, being fair and judicious and all that. "If that's the sort of thing you like."

"So she is," I agreed, tiptoeing around the quicksand I sensed nearby. "You've met her?"

"I've seen her photo. She looks a lot like her regular model."

I remembered the dramatic fashion photos in Vera Slote's offices, and saw the general similarity. "I see what you mean."

"But remember"—and Bly did her fine Mae West parody— " 'I'm no model lady. A model's just an imitation of the real thing.' "

"I suppose you want me to come up and see you sometime," I said.

"I'd like you to come see Robinson sometime, is what I'd like."

"Something wrong?"

"I hate to say it, Sam," she said, sounding very somber and serious, "but he's the kind of actor who *constantly* rewrites his lines."

The only thing to do was laugh; I laughed.

"Now, this is serious," she insisted. "He keeps coming up with his own material, and darn it, it's all from his old movies. He rides roughshod over me and Terence both."

"Terence?"

"Terence Whitehill, our director. We just can't get him to do the material in the script. 'I happen to *know*,' he says, and off he goes again. Sam, how much longer are you going to be in New York?"

"I have no idea. I guess . . . Well, I guess I can't go on with this business forever. But what am I supposed to do about Robinson?"

"Maybe you could call him," she suggested. "At home this evening? Do you think you could?"

"And tell him to be good?"

"He'd listen to you, Sam."

"I don't see why," I said. "He's never listened to me before."

"Will you try? Will you at least try?"

"You could always replace him," I said hopefully.

"Well, the thing is, Sam, he's good," she said. "He's awfully damn good; he sparks the other players and he finds things in the characterization that *I* never put there, I can tell you. When I think of the waste of him, all that talent, years and years just stuck in that house."

She'd never said that about *me*, an observation that bamboo shoots under my fingernails could not have forced me to admit out loud, not to Bly. "I'll talk to him," I promised. "I won't do any good, but I'll try."

"Thanks, Sam. Oh-oh, *such* watch! I'll be late for work! If you need me, whistle."

I whistled, but she'd already hung up.

41

I was a bit late to Vitto Impero. Anita and Bill were grinning and jawing away at each other at the table back by the kitchen—Anita, of course, wouldn't pull rank and give herself a *good* table—and as I moved toward them through the lunchtime crowd, I had a chance for a moment to look at these two friends unobserved—to kibitz their lives, as it were. Anita could smile at somebody other than me; Bill could turn his amiability and charm toward someone with whom he wasn't a fan. Each of us is an infinite number of people, changing and adjusting and altering slightly with every shift in the cast around us. My arrival would make Anita a different Anita, Bill a different Bill. And I would be different from the person who'd walked over through the Village in June sunshine thinking about murder and betrayal.

Their faces both smiled when they looked up and saw me coming. Bottles of San Pellegrino and Pinot Grigio were on the table, and before I'd even sat down, Anita had poured water into the larger glass at my place, and Bill, wine into the other. "Sorry I'm late," I said, taking my chair, my back to the room, a useful precaution in public places when I'd rather not be interrupted. "The phone hung me up."

"We didn't miss you at all," Bill told me, and toasted me in San Pellegrino. "Cheers."

"Same to you, fella." The water was fresh and cool after my walk. "One of the calls was from Vera Slote," I told him.

He was surprised. "She's back? I thought she wasn't due till Monday."

"Just arrived, got my message, phoned me. We're meeting for drinks tomorrow."

"Terrific! Where? What time?"

A socially delicate moment, this. Should I tell him bluntly that Vera was prepared not to see him again? Or let her cut him off her own way, in her own good time. I said, "We agreed, it should just be the two of us. Because of the subject matter, you know."

"Oh. Sure." He nodded, accepting that, then patted a brown paper parcel beside his place. "Tapes," he said, with an unaccustomed shyness. "For you to sign, you know. Whenever."

Oh, yes; the cutting edge of fandom. "Right," I said. Turning, I put my hand over Anita's on the table and said, "Hello."

"Yes, I am here," she said. "That's right."

"How are you?"

"Getting over my trip to Brazil."

I laughed, but said, "I kind of liked it."

Bill said, "I hate it when I don't know what people are talking about."

So that led into a description of last night's dinner at the Henderson's, which led inevitably into the inevitable subject: Doug Walford's death, and where-were-you. I told him about the elimination of four of my suspects, and between us, Anita and I filled him in on the movements of the other six, as so far established. Roughly, it seemed that at ten o'clock, when Doug was starting upstairs, Anita and Nora Henderson were talking together, while Jerry Henderson, Maria Kaiser, Terry Young, and Vera Slote made a foursome, discussing photography. Ten minutes later, Anita was with Robinson getting a drink, Nora and Jerry Henderson were together discussing departure, Maria and Terry were back together (having separated while Maria went upstairs to the bathroom), and Vera was with the Gretchen Young group.

It was the movement in between those outside times that was fuzzy. When the photography discussion broke up, Jerry Henderson joined his wife and Anita, and Anita then went to the bar. What was the time frame there? Was it long enough for Anita to have gone upstairs and come back down, between leaving the Hendersons and getting on line behind Terry? Did one or both Hendersons go upstairs after Anita left? If so, were they in it together, or not?

The same fuzziness confused the movements of the other three: Terry and Vera and Maria. We *knew* Maria had gone upstairs, and was seen by Ann coming back down. Was she lying when she said there was already someone in the second-floor bathroom, with the water running and the sounds of a person moving around? Did Terry have time to commit murder between leaving Maria and going to the bar, just ahead of Anita? Did Vera have time, between leaving the photography group and joining the Gretchen Young group? With any luck, Vera herself would be able to fill a bit more of that in when I saw her tomorrow.

In and around all this description, from both Anita and me, with occasional questions and suggestions from Bill, lunch was served. I assume it was delicious, since Anita does run a first-rate restaurant, but I didn't taste much—I was too involved in what I was saying and thinking. Over espresso, at the end, Bill asked me if I had any gut feelings yet about the guilty person, and Anita said, "Gut feelings? That's man talk for intuition, isn't it?"

Bill rolled with all punches, smiling and self-deprecatory. "Okay, you win," he said. "Intuition. Well, Sam? Any intuitions?"

"Not exactly," I said slowly.

"Oh," he said, studying my face. He made come-here hand movements. "Tell."

"Well," I said, with a look toward Anita, "it was last night—"

"I know," Anita said, nodding. "I know exactly what you mean, that struck me, too."

"*Both* of you," Bill said, with a great show of frustration. "Is this Brazil again?"

"In a way," I said.

"Motive," Anita said.

I nodded. "That's right." I told Bill, "Last night, Jerry Henderson gave a kind of explanation, or excuse, or whatever you want to call it, for whoever did this thing. The guy didn't know what it was going to be, is what it comes down to."

Bill looked startled. "Didn't know? What do you mean, didn't know?"

"Just that."

Anita said, "The idea was, whoever put the pressure on, at first they weren't demanding a murder, but just something less . . . less dangerous, or less important, or less—"

"Repugnant," I said.

"All right, good," Anita said, nodding at me. "Less repugnant."

Bill shook his head. "Such as?"

"I don't know," I said. "Steal my Rolodex, maybe; you

could probably get a few hundred for that from the *National Enquirer.*"

"Hardly that," Anita said.

"They once paid two dollars and fifty cents a name for Johnny Carson's Rolodex," I pointed out.

Anita laughed and patted my hand. "I'm not arguing your celebrity, sweetheart," she said. "I just mean, it would always have to be something mob-oriented. Right from the beginning, it would have to be a slide toward the big crime, so by the time the person realizes what's going on, it's too late to back out."

"I don't quite see the mechanism," Bill said, "but all right, as a theory. So?"

"So that was Jerry's suggestion," I said. "Sympathy for the murderer. I think he even said something like that, or maybe I did, and he agreed with it."

"Sympathy for the murderer." Bill frowned, first at Anita and then at me. "An explanation, you mean. How it could be a friend of yours, and still happen."

"Right."

Slowly Bill nodded, saying, "All right, possibly. It does make more sense that way, makes it easier to understand how an otherwise decent person could get into"—he waved a hand—"all this. How he could be drawn in, sucked down, never really wanting it to happen." Then he looked at me again, and a further thought struck him. "Oh," he said.

"That's right," Anita told him. "They were both high at the time, after dinner."

"Sam?" he said. "You think he was apologizing? You think he was offering an explanation about *himself?*"

I looked down to watch my fingers toy with the slice of lemon rind in the saucer. I swirled it in the black expresso, and faint oil lines trailed behind it, making no pattern. "I don't know," I said.

42

After lunch, I picked up a tan Mercury from the car rental place on 56th Street, took the Lincoln tunnel to the New Jersey Turnpike extension, and headed south toward Atlantic City.

It would be my first time there. Back during the days of PACKARD, I'd been to Las Vegas a few times in connection with various promotions, and had never much liked it. Las Vegas is merely another low, drab, sun-baked stucco flatlands town—America has a thousand such, and I've probably seen the shopping centers of a quarter of them—but that one has a hot glittering diseased tumor sticking up in the middle of it. Get a high-floor suite in one of the Strip hotels and look out the window and you see that you're merely in one of a cluster of Crackerjack boxes surrounded by flat-roofed grammar schools and crowded-together trailer camps on a dry flat desert with a circle of low hills at a distance all around, as though this were the world's largest and most filled-in meteor crater. I once heard someone describe Las Vegas as a city built in an ashtray, and that about sums it up.

But Atlantic City? It has a long and semiraffish history as a seaside resort, extending well back into the nineteenth century. Unlike the dry desert of Las Vegas, there was already something *there* in Atlantic City before the casinos lifted up their cobra heads beside the sea. Driving down through the three stages of New Jersey—noxious chemical plants, rolling greenery, pine barrens—I was in a way looking forward to seeing the place, and sorry that the demands of the restaurant had kept Anita from coming along to share the experience. It should, I thought, be interesting.

I was wrong.

The first clue, looking back on it, was the parking lots along the expressway leading into town. The center mall of the highway was mile after mile of parking lots, all restricted to *employees* of the casinos, with shuttle buses to carry them between their cars and their work, and it seemed to me I saw more Pennsylvania than New Jersey license plates in those lots. But wouldn't most of the employees of the casinos come from Atlantic City and its neighboring villages? And if not, why not?

I saw why not when I got there. Atlantic City had not, after all, been a seaside resort to which casinos had been added. Atlantic City had been a corpse, on which the casinos had been grown. Driving through block after square block of desolation, I could see what had happened. Atlantic City, having long since lost its luster, had turned into one endless squalid slum. The casino builders had scraped away the mold in the final block before the ocean and laid an imitation of the Las Vegas strip in a ribbon on top of it. The slum behind the ribbon had not been changed any more than the ocean in front of it.

At least in Las Vegas you don't dance on graves.

I was depressed and irritated by the time I got to Neptune's Realm, and even the high kitsch of the trident-bearing mammoth statues to both sides of the whale's-mouth parking entrance didn't cheer me up. In fact, I didn't think anything *could* cheer me up, and then something did: Robin Corrigan.

In the belowground parking garage, I had been greeted with smooth efficiency only slightly undercut by the echoing sounds of squealing tires somewhere out of sight. I'd traded in the Mercury for a cardboard check and a uniformed bellboy, who insisted on carrying my one overnight bag and making chit-chat about the weather and my drive down while we waited for the elevator up to the lobby. It came at last, we went up one flight, the door slid open to royal blue and silver glitz, and there was Robin, grinning at me. "Samuel, you look gorgeous," he said, and told the bellboy, "We're all checked in and going straight up to twelve. Let me see." He consulted the plastic card I'd be using as a key and told the boy, "Twelve-forty."

"Yes, sir."

We three were alone in the elevator as it stroked upward. I told Robin he looked gorgeous, too, and he said, "I keep forgetting how *tall* you are. Or am I merely shrinking under the weight of responsibility?"

"You look absolutely fit, Robin," I told him.

He did, too. He'd be almost forty by now, maybe even a bit more, but he still looked as dewy and boyish as ever, a slender ruddy man of just about six feet, who wore silks and cashmeres in neutral colors, displayed his homosexuality only in the gracefulness of the hand gestures that accompanied his speech, and had never, never, never been known to lose his temper. He was a wonderful road manager because he was utterly and permanently unflappable; whoever was causing the trouble, and whatever the trouble might be, Robin would outlast it.

As we rode up toward the twelfth floor, I said, "How goes it here?" and he rolled his eyes slightly, turning away from the bellboy, saying quietly, "Unbe-*liev*-able."

"Oh?"

We reached twelve, the door slid open, the bellboy led the way. The corridor carpet was a rich dark blue with a repeated pattern of a large silver line drawing of Neptune seated on his throne, holding a trident, being waited on by a pair of large-breasted mermaids. The left wall was covered in light gray fabric—meant to be silver, I supposed—but the right wall was unpainted gray Sheetrock stroked and dotted with dry white joint compound. About a third of the doors stood open on unfinished rooms, and the hall was almost completely lined with rolls of carpeting inside their clear plastic sheaths. Robin, following the bellboy, looked back over his shoulder at me and gestured eloquently at the rolls of carpet. "I see," I said.

After a right turn, we were in a more finished area, and at the end was 1240, my suite. Robin tipped the bellboy before I could, shooed him out, turned to me, and said, "A sane human being. I can't tell you what a pleasure it is to gaze upon such a thing."

"Having a little trouble here, Robin?"

"*Trou*-ble! Would you believe this place has been open four *months?*" We were in the large living room of the suite, with a bank of windows facing the sea, and Robin went around behind the bar to open the refrigerator. "Well, *that's* good, anyway," he said.

"My San Pellegrino?"

"*And* wine. And orange juice, if you feel like it. And I made them throw in a bottle of Stolichnaya simply because I was feeling bitchy. Anything?"

"Not yet." I went over to the windows and looked down,

and the Atlantic City boardwalk was there, in the afternoon shadow of the hotel.

Robin came out from behind the bar. He said, "We've already found out the regular room service is faster than the VIP room service, if that tells you anything."

"A little disorganized."

"What a talent for understatement. Sandy's one floor up, leaving tooth marks in all the furniture. They don't have her *stool*, Sam."

"I don't get it."

"A stool," he explained. "A simple ordinary backless hip-high wooden stool, preferably black. They are bringing us barstools, with puffy purple vinyl backs and seats that swivel, and they weigh five thousand pounds. She drags the stool *around* with her, Sam, all over the stage; first, she works to this part of the room, then she works to *that* part of the room. I keep telling them, 'The lady isn't a *furniture mover.*' Would you believe? The booking was made last September, we're four hours to show time, and we don't have a stool." He leaned forward, confidential, amusing, and half whispered, "I believe we are trucking one in from Philadelphia."

"If anybody can get her the stool, Robin," I said, "you can."

"Not *me*, Sam. There's a manager in this hotel, and he's beginning to realize we're here."

I laughed. "I'm sure he is."

Robin smiled. He enjoyed himself—that was part of the secret of his success—and he never enjoyed himself more than when he had a lot of trouble to deal with. He said, "Now, let's talk about you."

"Sure."

An arrangement of sofas faced the bar, their backs to the view of the ocean. We sat at an angle to each other. I kicked my shoes off and put my feet up on the glass coffee table, and Robin said, "I'm sorry, Sam, but I have to ask you to be up front with me."

"You want to know if my meeting Frank Althorn will make any trouble for your client."

"I want more than that, sweetheart," he said. "I want to know why, why, why."

I was ready, having realized Robin's protection of his client would include, if necessary, protecting her from me. If I were to tell him I wanted to meet Frank Althorn because I wanted to look at the man who'd ordered the murder of an old friend of mine, the deal would be off. I didn't like lying to Robin, but there wasn't much choice. I said, "Call it an actor's weirdness. I have a possibility for a guest shot on *Love Boat*."

"*Mazel tov*."

"Thank you. I'm doing my best to break the Packard image, so this is a completely different kind of part. Do you remember Terry Young, the reporter on the *News*?"

"Very well," he said. "Bright, funny, useful, and an utter slob."

"You remember him. I told him the part I might play and said I wanted to meet somebody in real life like that, and he said Frank Althorn."

"Like what?"

I repeated Terry's description of Frank Althorn as the mob's *shabbas goy*, and he said, with some astonishment, "*You're* playing such a character?"

"People said the same thing when I was cast as a criminologist."

He frowned. "You want to meet Frank Althorn because he's a mobster."

"I do not. I've seen mobsters. Althorn's a legitimate businessman who doesn't even hang out with mobsters, but he's helpful and useful to them." I gestured around the suite, meaning the whole hotel. "Like here, for instance."

Robin looked troubled. "Sam, I'm not sure Frank Althorn would enjoy being studied as that kind of role model."

"I wouldn't *say* such a thing to him! That's why it's supposed to be accidental. I'm really down here to meet Sandy Sheriff."

"Why?"

"A sitcom writer in Hollywood has a potential series for us; I'm wondering if she's interested."

"An actual existing sitcom writer, with credits and all that?"

"Absolutely. Her name is Bly Quinn. She has a pilot being shot on the Coast right now."

"And *does* she have a series for you and Sandy?"

"If I ask her to."

"Ask," he said.

It was then just after five o'clock; two o'clock in Los Angeles. "I'm not sure she's back from lunch yet," I said, "but I'll try."

There were two phones in the room: one on a small table by the sofas, and the other on the bar. I sat on the sofa to call Bly's studio number, and Robin went over to the bar to pour us both glasses of San Pellegrino. He brought me mine while I asked the receptionist for Bly, then went back to sit at the bar. When I heard Bly's voice, I gestured for Robin to pick up the other extension, which he did while I said, "Hi. It's me, Sam, in Atlantic City."

"Did you talk to Robinson?"

"Not yet, but I will. I want to get the other part organized first. Now, don't say anything until I'm finished."

"Why not?"

"Bly, just wait for it, all right?" I talked very fast. "This is about your series idea for Sandy Sheriff and me, and it's

why I'm here now at Neptune's Realm, where Sandy's appearing, because I'm going to meet her tonight. But I won't
mention the series idea yet.''

"Oh, you won't?'' She sounded a bit glazed.

"I just want to see how we get along. Being locked
together on a series with somebody where you don't get
along together can be the worst. So this is just to see how the
gears mesh.''

"Oh, they're meshing,'' she told me. "Sandy Sheriff and
Sam Holt. Not since Wallace Beery and Rin Tin Tin.''

"Well, it was your idea,'' I said.

"I've got a million of them. And here's the next. I'll put
Robinson on.''

"Bly, wait!'' But she was gone. I looked helplessly across
at Robin, who grinned back, amused at me.

The next voice I heard was Robinson's, saying, "You
called?''

"Very funny. Bly tells me you're rewriting her and it hurts
her very deeply, and she wanted me to mention it to you
because you probably don't realize how important it is to
her.''

"Yes,'' he said judiciously, "I'd been expecting she would
bring you in next. Was there anything else?''

"Robinson, what are you going to do about this?''

"My best for the program, obviously. I must go. I'm
being called to the set.''

"Talk to you later, Robinson,'' I said, and listened to the
click, and hung up.

Robin also hung up, saying, "Who was that?''

"An actor friend. And before that, the writer.''

Smiling, he shook his head at me. "You didn't coach her
beforehand. Lucky for you she's quick.''

"Quick enough?''

"Sandy's dying to meet you, between shows," he said, and headed for the door.

"Thanks, Robin."

He opened the door, looked back at me, and said, "One word of advice."

"Yes?"

"If you'll want breakfast in the morning, order it now."

43

They found her a stool, a black one, and Sandy Sheriff, a tall skinny blonde with gawky knees and elbows, dragged it back and forth on stage behind her, occasionally sitting on it, at times leaping from it, all the while she harangued her audience, who loved her. She talked very fast at top volume, she yelled and screamed and flung her arms around and wrestled with the stool, and I would say she used up more energy in fifty minutes on that stage than I do in a week in my gym at home in Los Angeles; and this was the first of two shows tonight. Her material was somewhat blue, but it was mostly an inflamed report of her ongoing gun battle with the world around her: arguments with cabdrivers and telephone operators, put-downs from agents and movie stars, struggles with pets and locked doors and income-tax forms.

The room was about three-quarters full, but the rest of her shows for the weekend were already sold out. At the beginning, she introduced the three celebrities in the audience—a sullen tennis player, a good-looking blond news announcer, and, lastly, me—giving each of us a gracious comment and leading the audience's applause. As I finished my bow and sat down, she said, "Listen, Packard, if I die up here"—and she pointed at the audience—"*they* did it."

She didn't die. Her audience loved her brashness and unself-consciousness and feistiness, and the material was quick and funny. Afterward, a security man led me back through the kitchens and netherworld hallways to her dressing room, which was actually an interior windowless suite behind the stage. Like the living room of my suite upstairs, its main room had a bar and an arrangement of sofas and a round table and chairs to one side for a dining area. A skinny rawboned woman let me in, and Robin waved languidly from one of the sofas, where he sat at his ease, knees crossed and foot gently bobbing as he steadily ate mixed nuts from a wooden bowl. The rawboned woman was introduced as Mary, the star's dresser, and the narrow little man making drinks at the bar was David, the hairstylist. The rumpled young man seated at the table with notepad and pen was introduced as Eddie. "Hiya," he said.

"Fine."

He said, very seriously. "Do you know the only place in this town to find a cherry is a slot machine?"

"Or a banana split," I said.

He frowned, and crossed something off on his notepad.

Robin said, "Sandy's in the shower; she'll be right out."

"Okay."

"I'll tell you how bad inflation is," Eddie said to me. "I went to the bank today to cash a twenty-dollar check, by the time I got to the front of the line it was only worth eighteen-fifty."

I said, "Is that how much you got, or is that the date of the joke?"

"Personally, I hate comedy," he said, pocketing the notebook and getting to his feet. "Look what it did to Rudolf Hess."

Why did that strike me funny? It was merely a non sequitur, delivered deadpan, but it surprised me and I laughed. Eddie gave me a jaundiced look. "It's too late to make it up to me," he said, and turned to Robin. "Tell Sandy this Jew will see her later."

"Okay, Eddie."

He gave me another look. "When it comes to women," he said, "you may be tall, handsome, rich, and famous, but I've got a gun." And he left.

David the hairstylist asked me what I wanted to drink. Jack Daniel's was among the bottles behind the bar, so I had some of that with soda. Robin said, "You want to din-din after? When Sandy goes back on, around twelve."

"Sure."

He paused in eating mixed nuts to call the Seven Seas Room: "This is Robin Corrigan, Sandy Sheriff's manager. We'd like two at midnight. No, not Miss Sheriff, she wouldn't eat in a joint like this." He hung up, laughing, and told me, "Sandy never eats. Or she always eats. I'm not sure which it is. No sit-down meals, anyway."

There was a knock on the door, Mary the dresser opened it, and four people came in. There was no question in my mind which one was Frank Althorn. He looked to be in his mid-fifties, somewhat burly, expensively and conservatively dressed, but wearing a large pinkie ring with a red stone. His watch's gold expansion band was over an inch wide, and his dark blue figured tie was held in place with a diamond stickpin. His hair was salt-and-pepper gray, thin on top and barbered neat and short around the sides. His ears were small and close to his head. He had Nixon-like jowls and a heavy dissatisfied mouth, but his forehead was large and smooth and clear, and his eyes were mild and almost puzzled-looking.

The bottom half of his face was a thug's; the top half, a saint's. His blunt-fingered hands were very pale, as though he washed them a lot.

The young woman with him was tall, nearly matching his six feet. She was about thirty, and looked a lot like the blond news announcer who'd been one of the celebrities introduced in the showroom. She was dressed tastefully and without overt sexuality, and when we were introduced (she was Margo), she shook my hand firmly, looking directly at me from level hazel eyes. The bimbos have learned that the johns like college girls, and the customer is always right.

The other couple were Sid and Ellen Feldman, a businessman of about sixty and his first and only wife. Sid was overeager, scared and trying to hide it with blustery good fellowship; when we shook, his hand was damp. Stout Ellen was just happy to be here, to be alive, to be rich, and not to be an ex-wife. "What an unexpected pleasure," she told me, taking my hand in both her soft pudgy paws. "I'm your biggest fan."

"Thank you."

David the hairdresser took drink orders, Robin explained that Sandy would be out of the shower soon, and Frank Althorn turned his innocent eyes on me, saying, "You've been off the tube a long time, Sam. Your fans miss you."

"We're working on a mystery story now," I told him.

"Good."

He would have turned away at that point, but I said, "I'd be interested to know what you think of the idea."

The innocent eyes showed a hint of wariness. "Me?"

"I'm not sure it plays," I explained. "It's a story about a man who's betrayed by one of his friends."

Althorn smiled faintly and shrugged. "Realistic enough," he said.

"The hero's hiding somebody in his house," I said. "No

one comes into the house but old and trusted friends, and yet somebody kills the fellow in hiding."

Althorn considered me. "Sounds like it's a story with a moral."

"Which moral?"

"Mind your own business." He shrugged again. "As the fella says, we pass this way but once."

"That's true."

"You're a long time dead."

"Also true," I agreed.

He smiled thinly. "How does the story end?"

"The guilty are punished."

"So much for realism," he said, and Sandy Sheriff came out of another room in a purple robe and a mink hat, shrieking hello at everybody, kissing cheeks and grasping hands, yelling at David the hairdresser that she was going to replace her hair with a plaster cast and he himself with a Cabbage Patch doll. She told Frank Althorn how fabulous his hotel was, and Frank grinned and nodded in obvious pleasure. "And the faucets!" she yelled, clutching both his wrists. "I finally noticed it, Frank, and all the fucking faucets are *dolphins!*"

"That's right," he said, nodding, now actually blushing. "It's Neptune's Realm, honey."

"It's fabulous, Frank, it's fabu-loso-loso-loso!"

When it was my turn, she grabbed my hand, pressed it to her bosom, fluttered her long black fake eyelashes up at me in a comic parody of sexiness, and said, "You and me in a series together! Robin told me *all!*"

Looking interested, Frank Althorn said to me, "Is that why you're here, Sam?"

"Partly."

"What a combo!" Sandy Sheriff said, still embracing my hand. "I'll play a mountain climber, and you"—she made her voice down and dirty, and ground her hips—"and *you'll* be the mountain."

44

Robin and I had an amusing dinner—I picked up plenty of show-biz anecdotes to relay to Bill Ackerson—and then he had to go back and see Sandy after her second show. "Shmooze the lady a little," he said, "before I fly."

"You're leaving tonight?"

"The Neptune Lear, out of Philly, at three-thirty. I'm opening the Brill Brothers in Miami tomorrow."

"That's a heavy schedule, Robin."

"Well, as Frank said, you're a long time dead." He cocked an eyebrow at me over our coffee and after-dinner Sambuca. "You did hear him say that, didn't you?"

"Yes, I did."

"Take care, my dear," he said. "I look terrible in black."

"I'll take care," I promised him.

We walked as far as the elevators together, and then he went on and I waited with four heavyset guys in short-sleeved polo shirts, talking about their evening at the crap table and the small changes in strategy that would have made all the difference. One of them carried a white vinyl bag with "Sun-World Tours" on it in block red lettering.

An elevator arrived, and we boarded. One of them pushed "9" and I pushed "12," the elevator started up, and the guy with the vinyl bag took out a black leather sap and swung it at my head. When I ducked, lifting my arms, another one kneed me in the groin. Meantime, another one was inserting a key in the control panel, turning it, stopping the elevator between floors.

I'm large, and I'm healthy, and I know one or two things about self-defense, but in a confined elevator against four professionals I didn't really stand a chance. And they were professionals, all right; their job was to make me hurt, without marring my face or breaking any of my bones or leaving me dead. Even though I managed to hurt them some, and did make one guy's nose bleed when I butted him, they never forgot their professionalism or the parameters of their task. Wearing leather gloves and wielding saps, all from that vinyl bag, they were the doctors, this was their operating room, and I was the patient.

They made me hurt. Yes, they did.

When they were finished, it was only the pain that was keeping me conscious. I was propped in a rear corner, crumpled up, vaguely aware of their feet. They got the elevator moving again, and exited at nine. They'd never said a word to me, not before or during or after, no threats or explanations or commentary of any kind. They themselves were the message, and I'd received it.

Those two tough guys back in San Francisco had tried delivering the same message, hadn't they? But they'd been less proficient at the job—just a couple of cheap day laborers— and that nice police car had just happened to come by at exactly the right instant.

No police cars in casino elevators. Pity.

Black and red spirals played in front of my face, trying to make me throw up. The elevator rose on up to 12, but how could I move? The door slid open, I saw dark gray trouser legs and black oxford shoes out there, and a voice I didn't know said, in disgust, "Christ almighty. Can't I let you out of my sight for a *second?*"

45

I lay naked in the outsized tub, the whirlpool attachment switched on, the too-hot water swirling around my aching body, bubbling under my chin. My rescuer sat on the toilet seat and viewed me with ironic detachment. He had helped me out of the elevator and guided my lurching steps down the carpet-littered corridor and unlocked my door with my plastic card and led me to the bathroom here, where the nice dinner I'd had with Robin did come up, while he started filling the tub. "An hour in here and you'll feel a lot better," he said.

It was ten minutes in the tub before I began to take enough interest in the world to actually look at this Good Samaritan, if that's what he was. He was about thirty, slender and rangy, with something southwestern in his speech and in the long line of his jaw. He wore a dark gray suit, a white shirt, and a dark red striped tie. He sucked Life Savers, and when he offered me one, I took it, since my mouth didn't taste very good. The sharp mint flavor revived me a little more; I peered at him and said, "If you don't mind my asking—"

He put a finger to his lips, and slowly shook his head.
Then he reached into his hip pocket, drew out his wallet,
opened it, and showed me his ID, a laminated card with his
photo, the name "Charles Petvich," and the information that
he was an employee of the United States Treasury Department. I nodded, painfully, and he grinned and put the wallet
away. I pointed to my ear and then to the nearest wall—it
was tiled, with bare-breasted mermaids on some of the tiles—
and he spread his hands, shrugging. Who knew, he was
saying, but why take chances? I nodded, and he went away,
and came back a few minutes later with a drink: vodka and
orange juice. "I don't think so," I said.

"I know so," he told me.

So I drank it, and he was right. He sat on the toilet seat
some more, and after a while I said, "I want to get out of
here."

"The tub, or the hotel?"

"Both."

"A good night's sleep—"

"At home," I said.

"Maybe you shouldn't drive yet."

"I don't want to be here, Charles."

He considered that. "I tell you what," he said. "You can
give me a lift to New York, and I'll do the driving."

"Good." Away from the walls with ears, maybe he'd tell
me why he'd entered my life.

He stood up, and stretched. "Be back in half an hour. You
want me to check you out?"

"There's nothing to check out," I said. "We just go."

"What about your bill?"

"No bill." The irony made me laugh, though it hurt to do
so. "They're comping me," I said. "I get all this for free."

46

The whole thing was too spookily reminiscent of my meeting with Doug Walford, back when he'd first called me. It was even the same kind of car. I'd carried my bag down to the parking garage a little after two in the morning, every muscle in my body on fire, and I saw no one. I reclaimed the Mercury, and by prearrangement met Treasury Agent Charles Petvich two blocks back from the hotel, where the street lighting was poor and the buildings that hadn't yet been torn down were either fire-gutted shells or desperate fortifications, sheathed in bars and gates. It took a brave man to stand there alone at that hour of night.

When I stopped, I slid over and he got behind the wheel. "You're right," I told him. "I am too stiff to drive."

"Tomorrow will be the fun day," he assured me. He adjusted the seat forward to suit his legs, and we followed the signs toward the expressway. I looked back, and the line of tall hotels along the seafront looked at first as though they were on fire. Or as though a war were going on, and the battle had already moved through this blasted terrain and was stalemated there on the beach.

We passed a shuttle bus delivering Resorts International employees to their cars outside town. I was sleepy and groggy and stiff, but I practiced isometrics as we rode, trying to protect myself from the tomorrow that Petvich had prophesied.

He didn't start talking until we were on the expressway, lining out westward, almost the only vehicle on the wide highway elevated over the swampy body of water known as Beach Thorofare. The hotels still glinted against the night behind us. Driving casually one-handed, his other hand resting on his leg, Petvich said, "Do you mind telling me how you got on Althorn's shit list?"

"Yes," I said.

He seemed mildly surprised at that. He glanced at me, then looked out the windshield again and said, "I see. You want me to go first."

"Yes, please."

"There is an ongoing investigation into Frank Althorn's activities," he said. "There are things we believe about him, but cannot prove. Maybe we never will; he's a careful man."

"Was that careful? To set his dogs on me?"

"Very careful. It means you're an annoyance but not a danger. He's letting you know to get out of his life *now*, before it becomes necessary to do something drastic. In the meantime, there's no visible damage, no witnesses, and no provable connection between Althorn and the people who worked you over. Maybe they were just tourists, sore at losing at the tables, taking it out on a stranger."

"A measured response, in other words."

"Exactly." He grinned a little, the dashboard light dramatizing his face. "I wouldn't have thought it was that easy to cut a celebrity out of the herd like that. Althorn knew he could, and did.''

"It's not like I'm the president," I pointed out. "Or even a currently working hotshot. Ex-series stars are a dime a dozen."

"Not quite. But the point is that Althorn let you know he's no respecter of persons."

Despite the isometrics, the stiffness was increasing. "I'll go along with that," I said.

"Your turn now."

"Not yet. You were watching me, or following me, or something. I remember what you said in the elevator."

"We knew you wanted to meet Althorn," he said, "that the meeting with Sandy Sheriff was just a cover."

"How on Earth did you know that?"

"Unimportant. What we didn't know was *why*, and that's what I'd like to hear about."

"Wait a minute," I said. "Back up a little. How did you know I wanted . . . Wait a minute, wait a minute." I was thinking hard.

Impatience made him grimace and give me a quick look. "Mr. Holt, you can't expect me to divulge private sources that have nothing to do with—"

"Oh," I said, getting it. "Robin Corrigan. Had to be. Nobody else knew . . . unless it's Harvey Mallon. But why would either of them—?"

"Mr. Holt, this really doesn't matter."

"Mallon would volunteer, if he knew you birds were around, but I don't suppose you'd let somebody like Mallon know what you were up to. But why would Robin . . . Of course, Sandy Sheriff *is* a currently working hotshot. Robin has a lot of clients, that is, Garson/Modell has a lot of clients who might be in a mutual back-scratching situation with the government. With the Treasury Department. What is it you people cover? Alcohol, Tobacco, and Firearms, right?''

"Yes, Mr. Holt," he said, sounding weary.

"And the IRS, of course. And Customs." I laughed, which made my ribs ache. "I wouldn't be surprised," I said, "if Garson/Modell kept an employee permanently stationed in your waiting room down there in Washington, with a briefcase full of explanations."

"Are you finished, Mr. Holt?"

"Nod once for yes. It was Robin Corrigan."

"I am not going to nod, Mr. Holt."

He wasn't, either. Past a certain invisible line, we weren't going to be buddies. My amusement drained away, leaving me merely tired and achy, but glad I at least had the sense not to mention I used to be a cop myself. As for Robin—his job is to service and protect his clients, not do favors for casual acquaintances out of the past. He's good, he's smooth, he knows his job.

And do I? "Wait a minute," I said. "What about San Francisco?"

He frowned at me. "San Francisco? I'm not following you."

He sounded bewildered enough, but it *had* to be connected; this whole thing had to lace together. I said, "Have you ever heard of Okushiri International Forwarding?"

"As a matter of fact, I have," he said, in some surprise. "But how do *you* know it?"

"I was in San Francisco," I told him, "asking some questions about Okushiri, and a couple guys came along and offered to do what Althorn's pals did tonight. Except those two were more amateurish, and a black-and-white just happened along in the nick of time."

"Instead of me," he said, "who happened along just *after* the nick of time."

"This isn't a coincidence," I insisted.

"Of course it isn't. *You're* the only coincidence in the story," he said, sounding annoyed. "Okushiri is a very small and minor link with Frank Althorn, one part of a whole West Coast shipping arrangement we're also looking into. Maybe our agent in charge out there saw you poking around, saw you were about to get your head handed to you, and sent some reinforcements. I wouldn't know. But what I *do* know, Mr. Holt," he said, giving me a severe look in the green-tinged light, "is that it's time you told me what the hell you're up to with all this poking and prying and offering yourself as a sacrificial victim."

"I think you're right," I said, and while we continued to run northward through the night, up the narrow spine of New Jersey toward New York, I did my isometrics while I told Petvich the story of Doug Walford, from beginning to end. He asked one or two questions, but mostly let me just tell my tale, and at the finish he said, "I think I agree with you. One of the six remaining people on your list was the trigger."

"And Frank Althorn was the hand."

"But what did you hope to gain by meeting him?"

"Nothing. I know I can't touch him. I want to find the person who came into my house and did that thing, not even to turn him in, because what can I prove?"

"What, then?"

"I want him to know I know. I want him to know he isn't welcome anymore."

For the first time, I heard Charles Petvich laugh. "Dumb," he said, "but understandable. And really all you wanted from Frank Althorn was to look at him."

"And let him know I know."

He shook his head. "I guess you did that, all right."

"Dumb again, eh? What would you think would be smart, Mr. Petvich?"

"I wasn't putting you down," he said. "When violence comes in and the tough guys are there, walking on your head and following their own agenda, what kind of reaction *isn't* dumb?"

"Doing nothing, I suppose."

"A bunch of years ago," he said, "in Baltimore, two mob factions were in a dispute. One side owned a brewery, and some guys from the other side went in there one night and loosened the lug nuts on the wheels on the delivery trucks. One of the trucks was on the Beltway, the left front tire came off, bounced across the lanes, and went through the windshield of a car coming the other way."

"Ouch," I said.

"My Aunt Helen was driving; she was forty-one years old. Nobody set out to kill her, but she was dead. My uncle just aged down to nothing; he lasted three years. He kept saying, 'What should I have done?' He told me once, there was a thing in the paper about one of the mobsters. He found out the guy had a daughter; he actually drove around behind the daughter sometimes, going to school and this and that. He was going to kill the daughter, see how the mobster liked *that*."

"But he didn't."

"He couldn't bring himself to." Petvich had both hands on the steering wheel now, and no expression in his voice. "What would you call dumb in that situation?" he asked. "To kill the daughter? To think of it and not do it? Or not even to think of it? Or what? After the tire went through the windshield, what was Uncle Danny's smart move?"

"What's my smart move?" I asked him.

"Your least dumb move," he said, "is we join forces. You find your killer, let us make him bird-dog the way to Frank Althorn. Deal?"

"Was it really your aunt and uncle?" I asked him.

"It really happened," he said.

I laughed. "I love bullshit artists," I told him. "We have a deal. And there's a certain congressman I'd like you to meet."

47

Bill Ackerson almost cried, looking at the X rays. "You have small cracks in three ribs," he said. "You have a whole lot of trauma throughout your torso. And if I took an X ray of your head, I'm pretty sure I'd find rocks."

"Okay, Bill." I'd started this morning very stiff, and when I'd tried to work the stiffness out in the lap pool, some of the chest pains became so sharp that I'd decided maybe it wouldn't be a bad idea to get some medical advice. On the phone, Bill had advised me to keep moving but without too much exertion, and come in to see him at ten-thirty, which I did. And now he was looking at X rays in the examining room with all the autographed celebrity photos around on the walls, and he was not happy with me. "You haven't asked my advice on the other thing," he said. "Investigating your friend's death. But this"—he waved an X ray at me, and it went *fwong-fwong*, like an old-fashioned thunder sheet—"is what you get. Why in Christ's name did you go see Frank Althorn?"

"To look at him."

Bill perched on the edge of the table. I was sitting up on the examining couch, stripped to the waist, blue and purple and yellow bruises all over me. Bill said, "This counts as medical advice, Sam. Doug Walford has been dead for a month. A medical examiner and a coroner agreed it wasn't murder. No police force is investigating the case. You're the only one making a fuss, and it isn't doing anybody any good, especially *you*. All that's happened so far is, you've alienated half your friends and got yourself beat up. I haven't wanted to say this, because I knew it was important to you, but now I'm saying it. Forget it, Sam."

"No," I said.

He shook his head at me. "Doug Walford wasn't worth it. He was a very ambiguous guy; you've said so yourself. You've got nothing to gain here, but you've still got things left to lose. Do you want Althorn killing *you*?"

"No."

"Go back to California," he said. "This is absolutely top-quality medical advice. Go to California, get yourself involved in some sort of acting job—"

"Hah."

"Then find a *hobby*, Sam. Don't, don't, don't shoot yourself in the foot anymore."

"Thank you, Bill," I said. "Can I put my shirt on now?"

"Yes. I'll give you two prescriptions to be filled: for pain and to help you sleep tonight. You shouldn't drink for a while; alcohol just brings the blood up to the surface of the skin, where the bruises are. What we want to do is dissipate the broken blood vessels that give you the discoloration."

"Okay."

He watched me button my shirt. "What are you going to do?" he asked.

I was going to go talk to a congressman and a Treasury

agent about murder and conspiracy, but that wasn't what my doctor would like to hear. "Well," I said, "at five-thirty I'm meeting Vera Slote for drinks. I guess mine will be San Pellegrino."

48

The T-man and the congressman met like cats, moving warily toward each other in slantwise fashion, sniffing the air, eyeing each other in quick sidelong stares. Is this stranger, their manner showed, who has undoubted power in an area away from mine, going to be an ally or an enemy? Will he be an obstructionist? Will he be a glory hog? Can I trust him? What's in it for me?

It has been said that one of the best exercises for an actor is simple observation of other people. After watching Charles Petvich and Don Toomey get to know each other, there were a number of startling roles I now felt equipped to play.

We met after lunch, in my house, neutral territory. I played host for a while—Petvich took coffee, black, Toomey tea with milk and sweetener, I San Pellegrino—and then we sat in the living room to get acquainted; a prickly affair. I began the process, by telling each what I knew about the other, and then Dan Toomey made his dumping-on-the-Third-World speech again—Uruguay and Uganda showed up in tandem, on schedule—and Petvich responded with a lot of murky stuff about "ongoing investigations," and "not ready for public airing," and "going up against a number of vested interests," and on and on. Toomey allowed as how he was going up against some vested interests himself, and for a while it looked as though nothing would be accomplished at all, as though these two would just settle for a bragging-and-complaining contest and go away without either having gained any marbles because neither would have played any.

Toomey finally broke the impasse by naming some names. Senator This, Representative That, a lobbyist called such and such, a Washington lawyer from thus-and-so major firm, and this is the support or encouragement they'd offered him, and this is what happened when he'd tried to follow through. Petvich, a man whose style was to play the cards so close to his chest that red and black ink came off on his shirt, finally unlimbered a bit after that, and admitted that one or two of the names Toomey had mentioned were also of interest to his department's "ongoing investigation." So that was a break-through of sorts, though Petvich did immediately go on to say, "I'm not the man in charge, you know. I don't have the authorization to name too many names or promise much assistance from the department. I'd have to clear all that with my bosses in Washington."

Toomey said, dryly, "I imagine I might know your bosses in Washington."

"You can use my phone if you want," I told Petvich, since I was growing tired of his determination to protect his virginity.

After that, though, Petvich did unbend, and he and Toomey had what in political circles is known as a "full, free, and frank discussion." Meaning, they didn't love each other, but they did see profit in cooperation.

What it finally came down to was, we were the three blind

men describing the elephant. Toomey's attention and concern had been limited to improper actions and influence by some pharmaceutical manufacturers, and their link with federal government. Petvich and the Treasury Department's investigation was centered on mob infiltration of legitimate businesses, ranging from construction to shipping. And I was the one saying it was all joined together somehow, but I didn't know how.

"That's the key, for us," Petvich said at last. "The connections. If we can *show* how they all come together in one pyramid, we can begin to break it down."

"And," Toomey said, "I'll have the leverage I need in the House, or at least a start."

"If only Doug had managed to get together with you two," I said, "it might have made a difference."

But Petvich shook his head. "Don't count on it. In the first place, who's going to listen to him? Loonies and paranoids wander in off the street every day."

"If you want to keep a high opinion of the human race," Toomey advised me, "never read a congressman's mail."

"The point is," Petvich said, "we're together now. I'll take these names and suggestions back to the department and convince the people there we should broaden the scope of our investigation." He made a downturning, sour smile. "They'll love that," he said.

"That's all good," Toomey said, "but I think the key, the best route into the heart of all this, is through the murder of Sam's friend."

"One way or another," I said, "the murderer must be an amateur, forced into the role. If we can find him—or if we can find *her*, that's still possible— If we can *prove* it, that's leverage to say, 'Who hired you? Who forced you?' "

Petvich said, "That's right. The end of the trail for you is the beginning of the trail for us."

"If I get to the end of the trail."

Toomey studied me, probably wondering just how frail a reed he was pinning his hopes on; or is that a mixed metaphor? Anyway, he said, "What do you think, Sam? You've narrowed your list of suspects. Can you bring it all the way down to one?"

"Probably not to prove in court," I said. "And maybe not at all. But I haven't used up the possibilities yet. I'm seeing another of my people later this afternoon. I don't want to spend the rest of my life doing this, but I don't want to give up either."

Petvich made his thin nonhumorous smile again. "None of us is going to give up, Mr. Holt," he said. He wasn't a politician, so he didn't have to call me Sam.

49

When the elevator door opened on six, I saw that Vera Slote was already in the waiting room, wearing a black linen dress and black high heels and carrying a large tan snakeskin briefcase. "Here he is now, Janet," she said to the motherly receptionist. "See you Monday." She crossed to the elevator, I held the door for her, and we rode down together.

She was really a very striking woman, Vera Slote, with her helmet of black hair shaped to her head, her already large almond eyes subtly emphasized by makeup, and her surprisingly generous and full-lipped mouth. Her nose was long and aquiline, her shoulders bony, her body long and lean and small-breasted. I hope it doesn't sound ungentlemanly to say so, but she made me think of some refined breed of dog: a Weimaraner, say, or a Russian wolfhound.

We walked to Fifth Avenue, chatting about nothing in particular, mostly the weather. June and October are the two best months in New York, and this June was living up to expectations: not yet too hot or too humid, with a high, clear, pale blue sky. Paris, she told me, was experiencing a depressing amount of rain this spring.

A place on Fifth Avenue with dark wood paneling was filled with office workers decompressing before heading home. To the rear were tables, each under its own imitation Tiffany shade. A few people recognized me as we made our way past the crowded bar, but nobody approached. I've noticed that people are more likely to leave me alone if I'm with a good-looking woman. Unless they're drunk, of course, but it was too early for that.

Vera had sherry on the rocks; I ordered San Pellegrino. She said, "You were drinking at your party."

"You noticed that?"

"I noticed my host, of course."

"I was in a minor accident, got some bruises," I explained. "The doctor told me to stop alcohol for a while."

"You *look* all right." The generous mouth smiled, and she studied me through her lashes—the real thing that Sandy Sheriff had parodied last night. The tip of Vera's tongue touched her teeth, then disappeared.

"It was all very minor," I said. "Like your bad weather in Paris. You haven't wilted at all."

"Thank you," she said, and smiled again, and sat back against the wooden booth. "I think sometimes about adding a line of men's wear," she said. "If all men were built like you, I'd be more tempted."

We grinned at each other, and I said something gallant, and we went on flirting till the drinks came. Lifting her sherry glass, Vera said, "To temptation."

"Sartorial?"

"To begin with."

We touched glasses and drank, and she looked at the small gold watch on her narrow wrist. "I really am sorry about this dinner engagement,'' she said. ''But it's one of those things, and simply can't be put off.''

''I appreciate the time,'' I said.

''I'm enjoying it.''

So was I, and I would have enjoyed it even more if I'd been sexually interested in Vera Slote. Well, no, wait a minute. I *was* sexually interested—I could hardly not be—but I knew I wasn't going to follow through, so it didn't seem kosher to push the flirtation into areas that promised more than I intended to deliver. Vera came on to me, and I kept it light, and after a while she shrugged, with a franker and less sexy smile, and said, ''To business.''

''I'm sorry,'' I said, ''am I being a bore?''

''Not at all. You're very sweet.'' The sexy smile came and went. ''I just thought, since your lady friend . . . Anita?''

''Yes, Anita.''

''Since she doesn't care about clothing,'' Vera said, ''I thought she might not be that important to you.'' Another shrug. ''A shallow viewpoint, I agree.''

''No, you're right. Anita doesn't care about clothing.'' And *I* don't care that she doesn't care, was the unspoken corollary.

''Well, no matter. There was something you wanted to talk to me about. Not, I hope, gift suggestions for Anita.''

I laughed, and the waitress came by, and after we'd agreed on another round, I said, ''It has to do with the party, and with my friend's death.''

''Oh, yes?''

''I'm trying to work out where everybody was for the few minutes before he was found.''

''Where everybody was? Why?''

''I have a theory of my own, about his death,'' I said, reluctant to mention murder in this setting, with this woman.

"People might have been where they could see things, or see other people, something like that."

She held her glass up and studied me over it. "You mean, you think the death was suspicious."

"Yes."

"Well. Possibly so." She sipped, put the glass down, and said, "That was a month ago."

"I realize that."

"I doubt many people will remember specific details a month later."

"Every little bit helps."

"My, my," she said, frowning past me, trying to think. "So much has happened in between."

"As I understand it," I said, to jog her memory, "at the end you were with a group of people talking about Europe. There was a man discussing exchange rates, two women who like to vacation together in Tuscany—"

"Oh, yes, yes! I remember. I had just gone to that group, actually."

"Yes? From where?"

"Next to you. You don't remember?"

Smiling, I said, "I think I'm in trouble."

"Not at all," she said. "I came over and stood next to you for, oh, no more than a minute or two. There was a group of you, listening to that actor fellow talk about . . . Well, that was the problem, I was never sure *what* he was talking about. I came in in the middle of the story, something about a mad industrialist, or a mad twin brother, or something—"

"It's the part Brett was playing on a soap opera."

"Oh, is *that* what it was. Well, you all were fascinated by it, and I couldn't make head or tails out of it, and Bill was there, too."

"Yes, he was."

"I thought he was coming around the group to talk to me, and . . . May I be frank about your friend Bill?"

I grinned and said, "I think you just were."

"Fine, then." She smiled, and gave me a level open-eyed look, and sipped at her sherry. "I left that group, and thought I might get myself another drink, but Anita got there ahead of me."

"To the bar, you mean."

"Yes. While I was with your group, my mind was wandering, and I noticed Anita talking with that very funny actress, Nora whatever her name is."

"Her stage name is Nora Battle."

"*That's* it. Just as I was leaving your group, Anita left Nora Battle, and there was already a line at the bar. She got there first, so I went over instead to the other group of people, talking about Europe."

I didn't say anything for a few seconds. I was absorbing this news, that here was someone who had seen Anita go directly from Nora to the bar, and that was the only part of Anita's movements that I hadn't been able to verify. My list had just shrunk to five, and I couldn't have been happier.

She peered at me. "Is something wrong?"

"Just the reverse," I said, and signaled the waitress. "I don't see," I told her, smiling, when she arrived, "why I shouldn't have Jack Daniel's and soda."

50

Finding the detail that totally and unequivocally cleared Anita had a major effect on me. I'd never really believed she could be the guilty one, but having it *proved*, having the last shred of doubt cleaned out of my brain, did make a difference. Some inner sense of urgency drained away, a hard knot of anger I'd been carrying around inside myself dissolved, and I remembered how to relax again. Anita and I had a fine and private Friday night, and when old friends invited me to come along as they opened their summer rental place out in East Hampton, I accepted without a second thought. We flew out Saturday morning in their little six-seater plane from Flushing Airport, and I didn't think about Doug Walford or my still-unknown false friend once all weekend. Saturday night there was a party, and Sunday we lay around with Bloody Marys and the *Times*. The ocean below the cliffs was not yet warm enough for swimming, but the rental property included a heated pool, which got its first workout of the year after lunch. I would have liked to join in, but the bruises on my torso were still too obvious, and I didn't feel like answering a lot of questions.

We flew back Sunday evening, I spent the night with Anita, and when I strolled back to my house around eleven Monday morning, there was a hefty package waiting for me from Harvey Mallon: the dossiers I'd commissioned.

I carried the package upstairs and left it for some time on my desk while I did other things. I'd paid ten thousand dollars for the contents of that package, and now I was reluctant to open it, disinclined to know the facts within it. When I finally realized how I was stalling, I forced myself to go back into the office, open the package, and take out the ten blue manila folders it contained, each one tied closed with a dark blue ribbon. The subject's name was neatly typed on a gummed label on each cover.

Much had happened in the last week, and half of these folders were no longer necessary. I tossed them into the wastebasket, then spread the other five on the desk, still tied shut, the names facing me. Jerry Henderson. Nora Henderson. Maria Kaiser. Vera Slote. Terry Young. Was it down to just these?

And did I really want to open these things? Did I want to know about Maria Kaiser's parents, Terry Young's credit rating, Vera Slote's marital history? Did I want to know if these folders contained abortions, indictments, divorces, psychiatric problems? I was looking for someone who had betrayed a friendship, but if I untied these folders, wouldn't that also betray friendships? Isn't it up to our friends to tell us as much as they want to about themselves?

I didn't open the folders. I stared at them a long time, remembering what my mind-set had been when I'd called Harvey Mallon and ordered them. I was thinking more clearly now.

Much more clearly. It had been there, inside my brain,

hidden from me only because I'd been looking in the wrong directions and not listening clearly enough. It had been there, but I hadn't known it until my mind gave it to me as a kind of gift, as a sort of reward, when I swept those other five folders into the trash as well. The blue parcels fell, filling the wastebasket, and the truth walked out in front of me and took a bow.

Two things had been said in my presence last week that would have told me, if only I'd been listening, who had done it and how it had been done. Either one of them by itself would have done the job, if I'd been paying attention. The answer was dumped in my lap twice, and it wasn't till I dumped those file folders in the trash that I saw it.

Her name was *Edna*.

Charles Petvich had told me I should get in touch with him through the Treasury Department offices in the World Trade Center. I picked up the phone and dialed.

51

Thursday was the earliest that everybody on my list was free for dinner, and even then we turned out to be one short. Bill had assured me earlier in the week that he would be able to bring Vera Slote with him, but on Thursday afternoon he phoned, sheepishly, to say he couldn't. "She's gone back to Paris, Sam. I'm sorry."

Given the attitude Vera had expressed toward Bill, this turn of events didn't surprise me. "Don't worry about it, Bill," I said. "Just come on your own."

"Shall I bring somebody else?"

"I'd rather you didn't. This is just for *us*, you know."

"I think I know what you have in mind," he said. "A group session, everybody listening to everybody else, looking for that one clue, that one discrepancy."

"Something like that."

"I'm sorry about Vera."

"She isn't necessary."

Bill wanted to talk some more, but all at once I was in a

hurry to get off the phone. I was up in my office, seated at the side of the desk that faces the window, which meant my back was to the door, and I was positive I'd just heard a sound in the downstairs hall. Had the door down there opened and closed? Was there someone down there, someone in the house? Allegedly, I was alone in here.

Was this a response to all the poking and prying I'd done? Had somebody decided that the little elevator ride I'd been given in Atlantic City wasn't message enough? Had the invitations to tonight's dinner produced one extra RSVP?

I still had my throwaway gun from when I'd been on the Mineola force. I'd never had to use one, thank God, and I had no idea if the thing worked, but I felt right now I'd be happier with a weapon in my hand, so I unlocked the bottom left drawer of my desk, and there it was.

An old High Standard Sentinel .22 revolver, it was scratched and battered, but with its snub-nosed little barrel and its smoothed-down quick-draw hammer and sights, it was ideal for the purpose for which I'd bought it, and for which I'd carried it in my sock on every tour for nearly a year back in Mineola. If ever I'd been in a situation where the adrenaline had been high and the tension strong and my reaction time a little too good, and if an alleged perp had been shot by me under what might have been considered dubious circumstances, this little beauty would have been found very near that fellow's hand. It had never happened, and I wouldn't ever want it to happen, but a throwaway gun is as vital to a policeman's self-defense as the legitimate revolver in the holster on his hip.

I had always kept three rounds in the cylinder, none of them under the hammer, so now I brought the first cartridge around into firing position before I noiselessly crossed the room and eased open the hall door.

It was midafternoon, a sunny day, but the interior hall at this level is always dark unless I turn the lights on, which I'd

neglected to do. In the dimness, a dark figure was coming up
the stairs, moving slowly but not with any apparent stealth.
With my two-handed grip the little pistol almost disappeared,
but I stood braced in the doorway, arms fully extended,
aiming at the back of that head, and just as I was about to
speak, he turned at the top of the stairs, and I found myself
sighting along the barrel at the extremely startled face of
Robinson.

Never at a loss, Robinson. "Well!" he said, recovering at
once, giving a flawless display of outraged dignity. "Now,
here's what I call a homecoming."

I lowered my arms and shook my head. "Robinson, Robinson," I said. "What the hell are *you* doing here?"

"I had thought I might be welcome," he informed me,
and made as though to return down the stairs, saying, "Apparently, I was wrong."

"Oh, don't be silly." The release of nervous tension had
made me irritable. "Come in and tell me what you're doing."

I turned my back on him and crossed the office to my desk
to lock the throwaway gun in its home in the bottom drawer.
Robinson, deciding to cut the comedy, followed me into the
room, and when I looked at him, he said, "Well, it was just
impossible, that's all."

"Akers' Acres."

"One begins to understand why situation comedy television is so dreadful."

"Robinson," I said, "did you *quit?*"

"I gave them my terms," he said coolly. "They refused to
accept. There was no room in their general schema for talent,
taste, or experience."

I can hardly wait, I thought, to hear Bly's side of this
story. I said, "So you gave them an ultimatum, and they said
no."

"And here I am. Being offered violence," he couldn't resist adding.

"Maybe you were better off out there," I suggested.

He didn't deign to respond to that one at all. Looking about, with a faintly curled lip, he said, "You haven't been surviving very well without me, have you? Just as well, I suppose, that I came back. Are there any social events on the agenda?"

"As a matter of fact," I told him, "we're having a dinner party tonight. I'm glad you're here, Robinson, because this is something a little special."

52

Anita was catering again, and the guest list included Terry and Gretchen Young; Jerry and Nora Henderson; Brett Burgess; Maria Kaiser; my lawyer, Morton Adler, with his wife, Agnes; Bill Ackerson; and Ann Goodman and Helen Mayhew. Thirteen of us, plus Robinson, who assisted Anita in the preparation with a chilly disdainful aloofness that she misread as the perfectly correct demeanor of the servant; where ignorance is bliss, it would be folly for *me* to put anybody wise.

Most of the guests had some idea that this wasn't an ordinary dinner party, that it was linked somehow to the death of Doug Walford, but to the questions that people asked as Robinson ushered each of them in, I merely returned a bland smile and the promise that everything would eventually come clear.

The wide doorway was open between the living room, where we gathered for predinner drinks, and the dining room, where the table was set as elaborately as my cupboard would allow. Anita, who had everything ready in the kitchen, was

with us, and Robinson moved among us refreshing drinks
and offering hors d'oeuvres.

We were all still in the living room, chatting quietly
together, when Gretchen, who had wandered through into the
dining room, called back to me, "Sam, I'm sorry, but this is
wrong."

Conversations faltered. People looked at Gretchen, or at
me. I said, "Wrong? In what way?"

"This table is only set for twelve," she said, "but there
are thirteen of us."

"One of us won't be staying," I said.

Well, I may be a mere television actor, lacking stage
experience, but I do know how to deliver a good line. I
couldn't have gotten more attention at that moment if I'd
announced I was the reincarnation of Vishnu. Everybody
gaped at me, and Terry Young said, "You don't mean it.
Sam? You *cracked* the goddamn thing?"

"Yes."

Jerry Henderson, who was looking a little flushed and
manic and who I believe had come to the party already
stoned, said, "Next, if I understand the way these things go,
you're going to tell us the murderer is someone in this
room."

"No, actually, I'm not," I said. "She couldn't make it
tonight, could she, Bill?"

Bill Ackerson stared at me, wide-eyed. "Don't do this,
Sam," he said.

"It's too late," I told him. "It was too late when you
started."

Maria Kaiser said, "That can't be right. It can't be right."
But everybody else just stood and listened.

"Sam," Bill said, patting the air, trying to put the evils
back in the box, "you don't know the situation, you don't
understand what—"

"As a matter of fact, I do," I said. "I gave your name to a fellow I know in the Treasury Department on Monday, and we understand a lot now. We know why you were the one when the mob was looking for some friend of mine with a handle on his back."

"Sam, not like this. Not in public."

"These are the people I doubted," I told him. "These are the friends I couldn't be sure of anymore, because of you. These are the people we both owe an apology."

Nora Henderson suddenly blurted forward, hands waggling, spilling her drink on the carpet. "I don't want this," she said. "Whatever it is, I don't want any of this."

I said, "Nora, it won't bounce back on you. The police can establish Bill as a supplier of cocaine to his show-biz patients without you and Jerry coming into it."

Bill sighed, like the air letting out of a balloon. He stumbled back a step, and sat on the morris chair, while Terry frowned at me, saying, "I don't get it, I don't see how it worked."

"Doug left this house a few times after I'd moved him in," I said. "He called his private-detective friends, he bought clothing after Anita fattened him up. One of those times, he was seen. The people who wanted him dead needed a way into my house, and Bill was the guy they found. They had a week or a little more to set things up."

Making gloomy sounds like a lawyer, Morton Adler said, "Sam, you may be risking some prosecutor's case here."

"I hope not," I told him. "Petvich, my Treasury Department man, says he's pretty sure nobody here will have to become involved, particularly if Bill cooperates and makes a statement."

We all looked at Bill, waiting for him to say whether or not he would cooperate and make a statement. He blinked around at the faces, none of them particularly hostile, but

none very friendly either. We're looking at him like a speci-
men, I thought, and despite myself, I felt sorry for him. He
looked this way and that, and then he frowned at me and
said, "Why? On *Monday?* What happened on Monday? How
did you—"

"How did I realize it was Vera?"

Brett suddenly said, "*Vera Slote*? Vera Slote isn't a
murderess!"

"Of course she isn't," I agreed. "On the other hand, the
woman Bill brought here wasn't Vera Slote. From my description, Petvich says the FBI thinks she's a woman called
Alice Kaye, who *is* a murderess. I had drinks with that
woman last Friday, and she told me to meet her at her office.
When I got there, she was in the waiting room, as though
she'd just come out, and she said so long to the receptionist
the way Vera Slote would have, saying, 'Good night, Janet,
see you next week.' But I'd been in that office before, and
the real Vera Slote's assistant had called that receptionist
Edna."

"*She* screwed it up," Bill said, looking angry and mulish.
"*She* did it wrong."

I said, "Bill, when I told you Jerry's theory, that the
murderer had been led in by easy stages, you were startled,
because that's what had happened to you. They didn't tell
you to bring a murderess into my house. What did they say?
What did you think was going on?"

He frowned. He looked agonized. Then his eyes met mine
and he looked deeply embarrassed. "Burglary," he said.

"Burglary?"

"She was supposed to be an expert, somebody who knew
antiques and valuable things. What they told me was—"

"I don't *believe* this!" Nora said.

"Hush," I told her. "Go on, Bill."

He said, "They told me she'd come in and look around

and do like an inventory, and if it seemed worthwhile, then somebody else would break in some other time. They . . . they could make a lot of trouble for me, Sam, if they wanted. And I figured, even if they burgle you, you're probably insured. And maybe they won't do it.''

''What a fine creep,'' Terry said.

Bill said, more forcefully, ''If I'd thought for a second . . . Jesus, Sam, when it happened, I didn't even make the connection! I believed the suicide, I really did! It was only afterward I thought, holy Christ, it had to be. And then you came back and you were asking all over the place, and I was just lucky the real Vera Slote was out of the country for a while. I went to those, you know, those people, and I told them you can't kill everybody. If you kill this famous TV star it's a big stink, and then you'll have to kill *me* because I'll go to the police, and there's no end to it that way. So they agreed that woman would come back—I never knew her name, except Vera—and we'd keep you from getting suspicious.'' He shook his head, angry again. ''She's better at killing, isn't she?''

''She pretended to be no longer interested in you,'' I said, ''so she could fade out of our lives. And you told her all the guest movements at the party that I'd traced out, so she could fit her own in, and even give me that story about watching Anita, because of course *Anita* was the one I most wanted to clear. And the person who gave me that was somebody I'd want to believe.''

Anita said, ''Bill, I don't understand how it got *started*. How could you even *begin* this?''

''I can tell you,'' Brett said.

We all looked over at him, surprised. Brett was lowering down at Bill, furious but under control. Staring Bill in the eye, he said, ''It's because Bill isn't your *friend*, Sam, he's a *fan*. Bill's a fan and you're a star, and to the fan the star isn't

real, he isn't human, he's something else entirely. Your
friends are real, and you wouldn't betray them, but you can't
really hurt a star. Can you, Bill?''

Bill said, looking at me, ''When you came in with the
bruises and the cracked ribs, and it's all because of what I let
get started, honest to God, I almost couldn't take it. I almost
told you right then in the office, but I was a coward. I wish I
had. I wish you'd found it out from me. I wish there wasn't
anything to *find* out.''

''Bill,'' I said, ''Mr. Petvich is waiting for you out front.''

He took a deep breath. He didn't meet anybody's eye.
''I'm sorry,'' he said.

Brett said, ''You want me to walk you to the door?''

I said, ''No, he doesn't need help.''

He didn't. He got up, still not looking at anybody, and
left. He went out of the room, and out of the house, and
closed the door.

It didn't feel like a victory, or an accomplishment. It didn't
feel like anything good at all. I looked around at my friends,
and saw my own feelings reflected. ''Well,'' I said. ''Probably we could use another drink before dinner. Robinson?''